BORN

THIS WAY

TAMMY FEREBEE

BORN THIS WAY

Copyright © 2018 by Tammy Ferebee

This is a work of fiction. Names, characters, businesses, places, events and incidents are either the products of the author's imagination or used in a fictitious manner. Any resemblance to actual persons, living or dead, or actual events is purely coincidental.

All rights reserved. No part of this publication may be reproduced, distributed, or transmitted in any form or by any means, including photocopying, recording, or other electronic or mechanical methods, without the prior written permission of the publisher, except in the case of brief quotations embodied in critical reviews and certain other noncommercial uses permitted by copyright law.

www.tammyferebee.com

Cover Design and Formatting by The Book Khaleesi
www.thebookkhaleesi.com

ISBN-10: 0-9966292-2-X
ISBN-13: 978-0-9966292-2-5

First Edition

10 9 8 7 6 5 4 3 2 1

Other Titles by Tammy Ferebee

OUTSIDERS

OUTSIDERS 2:
Unfinished Business

To every individual who feels inadequate,
undeserving, and unloved, I want you
to know that you aren't.
You are enough, you deserve happiness,
and you are loved.
I love you.

CHAPTER 1

On my back, I lie, tracing where the .22 caliber bullet hit me, penetrated my chest wall, and damaged my lung, almost killing me. I lie on the floor, behind the closed door, beneath the square wooden entrance to a space too small to be considered an attic, housing nothing but dust, wooden posts, and a pile of used tights. I lie beneath my hung clothing, where I spent last night and just about every other night for the past nine months. I lie in the small, lit, windowless space. The only place I feel somewhat safe.

Like every other morning, I awaken before my alarm sounds. I stand, give the light chain a firm yank, throw my tee back on, and walk back into the bedroom before my Aunt Linda comes in to announce that breakfast is ready.

On the side of the bed, I sit with my eyes down on my phone. The time on the screen reads 6:59. In seconds, the alarm will blare, and only a minute or so after, Aunt Linda will be at my door to make sure I'm awake and prepared to eat with her.

Over the course of the first few months I was here, she'd check in throughout the night, never getting a full restful night of sleep herself. She would come in several times to not only make sure I wasn't having nightmares, but to ensure that I was still alive. That period has faded, and I'm happy, for not only myself, but for her because she sleeps throughout the nights again.

My alarm blares, and I silence it immediately. I don't check the messages waiting for me. I know who they're from and what they say. One is from my mother, a Bible scripture to *start my morning off right.* The other is from my best friend, Nikki. I'm sure her message wishes me a good morning and reminds me that she'll be spending the afternoon here to support me before the trial begins tomorrow. Both replies can wait until after breakfast, until after the morning line of questions.

Aunt Linda taps the door softly. "Joseph? You decent?" Her southern accent is as sweet as her heart.

"Come on in."

Still sitting on the side of the bed, I watch as

she enters. My aunt smiles warmly, her hair hidden beneath her satin nightcap, and her nightgown hidden beneath her buttoned robe. "Good morning. You sleep well?"

I nod, giving her the same dishonest response I give her every morning. Whatever I tell her is shared with Dr. Benson, and I can't bear seeing him any more than I already do. He's supposed to be helping me recover. I have yet to understand how I'm supposed to do that when I have to see him multiple times a week, talk about what I'd rather forget about, and take medications that don't do what they're prescribed to do. I'm sure he's helped many others, but I've yet to see the benefits of my many visits, so I say and do whatever is necessary to keep from having to be in his office any more than I already am.

"You hungry?"

Not at all. "I could eat," I say, nodding again.

"Good. Food is on the table. I'll meet you in the kitchen."

I step into the bathroom and flush down my morning dose to avoid another case of miserable nausea. I prepare to face another day of anxiety, another day of repetitive questioning, another day of prayer, another day of lies, another day of hell.

I brush my teeth and splash a little water on my face, never giving my reflection so much as a glance before heading for the kitchen. The table is set for two. Scrapple, bacon, two buttermilk biscuits, and a mountain of scrambled eggs sit on both plates. She's waiting at her end. I sit at the other.

"I waited on you to help me bless the food."

Immediately, I lower my head and clasp my hands together. She wastes no time to begin praying. I recite her words, giving thanks for this food that's going to take nothing short of a miracle to get down.

"Amen!" she says loudly.

I whisper, "Amen."

I pick up my fork and start on my eggs.

"Take your medicine?"

I nod.

"You sure you slept okay? It's understandable if you didn't."

"I slept fine, Auntie."

"You don't look well." She drops her fork, stands, heads my way, places her hand on my forehead, something she's done countless times. It still stuns me that possibly being ill is the only reason she'll make physical contact with me.

With eggs on my fork, I wait for her to determine that I have no fever. I allow her to play doctor, babysitter, therapist, lawyer, and every other role she needs to assume in order to feel like she's taking the best care of me.

"You're not hot."

"That's because I'm not sick. I'm fine. Really," I say convincingly. "Please, eat your food."

"Maybe it's worry I'm seeing." She goes back to her end of the table. "Tomorrow is not going to be easy for you. It won't be easy for any of us."

I shove a forkful of egg in my mouth and begin chewing. *Don't talk with food in your mouth.* That's something I've heard for as long as I can remember. Though my growing anxiety has unsettled my stomach too much for it to growl for food, I need to eat for strength, and it also works as the perfect excuse to remain mute throughout this over-visited topic.

"Not guilty," she mumbles, shaking her head. "That sick man really thinks he stands a chance. Nobody on that jury is going to believe him for even a second." She sips some of her orange juice. "I reckon a sicko would gamble with his own freedom. Maybe he feels like because he can charm innocent, naïve teenaged boys, he can charm a jury into a favorable verdict."

My stomach churns. My body overheats as

though the room has become an instant sauna. I drop my fork, grab my glass, gulp down about half of my orange juice, swallowing large chunks of pulp with it.

"Joseph, you all right?"

I nod.

"You may not think so, but the trial will be the best therapy for you. Seeing that monster prosecuted is what you need. You need that more than the pills. Maybe even more than Dr. Benson. Justice, Joseph. You need to see justice served."

Sure I do, but whose version of justice?

She bites into one of her biscuits, and I bite into one of mine. As I chew, I look around at the wood paneling, at walls that make this house look its age and unpleasantly dark. Dr. Benson has talked to me many times about my environments having an effect on my feelings and moods. He should have a session with my Aunt Linda about that. The wood paneling, wood floors, and small, curtain-covered windows rob this place of any potential for brightness. Though a little sunlight creeps through, for some unknown reason, my aunt doesn't like her curtains moved unless she wants to let some air in. There are lamps in every room, but artificial light is no competition for natural sunlight. Unfortunately, my aunt doesn't understand, or maybe she doesn't care about what light will do for her home. Or for me. A couple of times, I've opened the curtains in an attempt to brighten my day, to try out Dr. Benson's advice, but minutes later she pulled them closed. She never took an angry tone with me, never yelled, never disciplined me southern style. In her sweet voice that sings of the south, she asked me to keep her house the way she requires. She prefers the beds perfectly made with quilts and not comforters. She's had the same red plaid curtains since before I was born, and they're not to ever be scrunched up. She also doesn't like dry clothing left hung on the clothesline for too long. We're well into the twenty-first century, but she insists on living like she's stuck in the fifties. She gives the church more than enough of her money. The congregation has made it possible for First Baptist Church to get remodeled twice, but she hasn't restored her walls, hasn't bought herself new furniture in years, and would be better off driving a lawnmower than that piece of shit car she has parked outside. All that matters to her is attending church and her religious décor. Every wall and almost every shelf holds a Christian portrait, figurine, cross, or framed scripture. Family photos are throughout the home, but if numbers told the story of her true experiences, you'd think she was a guest at the Last Supper.

Aunt Linda is sweet, and though I believe her heart is good, she's a special kind of ignorant, closed-minded individual, and she doesn't stand alone. First Baptist Church is full of them, and the pastor, my father, encourages his way of thinking which has become everyone else's.

She dabs the corners of her mouth with her napkin. "Is Nikolette still spending the afternoon with you?"

"Yes."

"I'll be over at the church for most of the day. We'd love to have you, both of you, actually. Your mom doesn't want to pressure you because of your anxiety, but it'd make her happy to see you in church again. It'd help you, too, in more ways than you think. Showing up, seeing your father, and sitting amongst your church family may be the best way to prepare for tomorrow. I know it'd mean something to your father. His silence and distance aren't meant to tell you he doesn't love you. I just don't think he knows how to approach you after all that's happened, or what to say about your confusion. Finally coming back and sitting through a service may be what's needed to break the ice."

Break the ice. My confusion. The ice has already been broken. Shattered actually. My father knows I'm gay. He heard the words come from my mouth. Nothing to be confused about. My sexuality is something he doesn't understand, that none of my family, none of the church members understand. Truthfully, it's something I don't understand either. I don't know why it was my life that had to be lived this way, made unimaginably difficult because of my attraction toward males. All I wish is that the people of this town would at least try to tolerate it. Not repel it, insult it, and be so hateful toward me.

My eyes look over my pile of eggs. Eggs as yellow as the faux mums lining the town pharmacy's front windows. I'm sure their purpose is to make the place appear welcoming, to brighten the spirits of patrons on their sick days. Bright flowers or not, to me, the pharmacy is just another black hole in this town.

A while back, I had dropped in to grab a pain reliever. A few of my not-so-friendly schoolmates had come in behind me and hung out in the aisle I was shopping in. As I browsed the shelf, trembling, fearing their cruel words and possibly a hit, they laughed.

"Fucking fag," one called out. I didn't turn to see which one, and really it didn't matter which. I just tried to focus through my fear on making a selection, so I could get out of there.

"You know you can't cure AIDS, right?" another one asked.

Still, I didn't turn around. I grabbed a bottle of pills and hurried away from them with my head lowered and moved toward the register where Mr. Wallace was writing on his clipboard.

"Good afternoon, Mr. Wallace. How are you?" I greeted.

As I had expected, he didn't look up from his clipboard, didn't acknowledge me at all. Had my father been present, standing at my side, those boys wouldn't have followed me in and Mr. Wallace would've pushed his opinion of me to the side and treated me like a human being. But I was alone. That made me a target.

I stood waiting. I could hear the footsteps and chuckles of the guys who were harassing me in the aisle. Behind me again, one asked, "Can't you see that he clearly doesn't want to help you? He doesn't want to touch something your gay ass touched. Nobody wants to catch AIDS."

He sounded so ignorant, so childish, so

harsh, and yet Mr. Wallace didn't tell him to be quiet, didn't demand that he watch his mouth, didn't ask them to leave, and didn't ring me up so I could escape the situation.

I began to shake violently, decided I could suffer through my headache, and left without buying the medication. I walked down the sidewalk, beneath the awnings, past the small, nearly identical brick-front shops all owned by people I grew up knowing and attending church with, and waited at the corner to cross the street. Across the way, I saw Mrs. Parks, an elder from my church who suddenly stopped speaking to me once the rumors about me started. Based on speculation, she had become one of many who began to irrevocably abhor me. The look she shot me, the repulsion in her eyes, forced my head down and made me take the long way home, questioning with each step how this could be my life.

I look up from my eggs, mentally rejoin Aunt Linda for breakfast, and shove more food in my mouth. While chewing, I feel myself desperate to emotionally fall apart. I'll never be able to make sense of how people who preach love and live in homes decorated to look like small chapels could spew such hate toward people who would never hurt another, people who just live differently than them. How can people who have watched me grow over the past eighteen years so instantly turn on me, falsely diagnose me, abandon me, want my life, the life of a gay man, but still a life nonetheless, to exist no more?

"Joseph, I asked you a question. Church? You and Nikolette?"

I shake my head. "Sorry, I got lost in thought for a second. We're just going to stay in, chat, and keep my anxiety down."

She cocks her head to one side.

"And pray," I rush to tell her before she can speak. "I'd like to pray, talk, and spend a quiet afternoon with my friend."

"Sounds relaxing," she says before sipping her juice. "That should be nice. Friendly support."

I continue to eat what I have no appetite for as I try to wrap my mind around how much things have changed. I remember when boys and girls spending alone time together was an inappropriate, unspeakable concept, but recently the idea of Nikki being alone with me has become acceptable. Almost encouraged at times. I think for my aunt and mother, it gives them hope. Maybe they've convinced themselves that Nikki can change me, that my beautiful, curvy, well-liked friend can fix me and end my *confusion.* I think they believe the keys to turning me straight, and unraveling what they feel are mixed up thoughts, are a combination of the justice system, the church, unending prayer, and the presence of Nikki. My aunt, my mother, this whole town refuses to believe that I've been gay for as long as I've been black, for as long as I've been alive. Bruce didn't warp my young mind. I didn't wake up one day and think this up. It's in me.

"Your mama will be by this evening. She wants to spend a little time with you to make sure you know you're supported before the trial begins. It may be a good idea to find out what time, so you can end your visit with Nikolette beforehand. I think it'd do you some good to spend the evening alone with your mother in an environment where you've begun to feel safe."

I nod with my mouth full.

"She doesn't come by often, but she loves you, Joseph. She just doesn't know how to deal with all that's happened. I don't think she knows how to be present for you and your father. A wife must honor her husband, and while you're their child, in many ways, they've lost the son they've raised and always known. They're trying to understand how to help you through this phase while keeping their union strong. Your father needs her there with him, but her heart is still with her child. She still loves you. She just can't abandon her role as a wife."

Just as a mother, I guess. For months, the news was focused on my story. Millions listened to or read about how a 56-year-old pervert built a virtual relationship with a naïve, sexually confused young man, crossed state lines to meet him, engaged in sexual activities, and ultimately shot him to prevent the innocent young man, *me,* from speaking out. My story, like most of the others circulating, is more fiction than fact, and in less than twenty-four hours, I'll be in the spotlight again, unsupported by my mother like before.

"You understand?" she asks.

"Yes," I say. "I'll find out what time she'll be by."

I continue to force feed myself as my aunt repeats to me how necessary it is that my mother remain at my father's side. She works her damnedest to tug at my heartstrings, to make me feel sympathetic about the position my parents have been forced into, to make me feel loved by parents I feel so abandoned and betrayed by. I listen, swallow, nod, offer the answers she needs to hear. I sit through another painful, one-way conversation that makes me, the victim, the one wounded by a gunshot, feel like the cause and center of everyone else's problems and pain. I sit waiting for my moment of relief, the moment when she'll notice the clock, stop talking, jump up from her seat, and begin rushing around to get dressed for Sunday service. I impatiently wait for her to leave the table, to bring silence back into my world, to leave me alone. Alone until Nikki arrives. Until I'm with the only person in my life who doesn't blame me or hate me for being gay.

CHAPTER 2

I sit on the couch. Images of Christ, his disciples, and my family members surround me, and an open bible lies on my lap. My aunt doesn't interrupt prayer for any reason. She will ignore the fact that I'm in the middle of a phone call, has at times talked to me through the bathroom door, but not once has she said anything to me, not even one word, while I'm reading the Bible or praying. Laying the Bible in front of me saves me from having to answer additional questions or from having to reject another invitation to church service. The open Bible sends a clear message that she never ignores, a message she responds to by leaving me to myself to hear God or talk to Him.

She enters the living room. I never lift my head to make eye contact with her. Instead, I squint my eyes, trying to appear deeply focused on a scripture. She never says a word, but turns and unlocks the front door. Dressed in her Sunday best, a blue skirt, matching jacket, and a large blue hat with a floral brim that'll surely earn her a ton of compliments, but block the view of whoever is seated behind her, she walks out the front door. Though I'm sure she's disappointed that I won't physically be in church, I know it touches her and warms her spirit to think I'm spending the day praying and reciting scriptures.

I exhale, close what I wasn't reading, and recline back into the cushions. Alone, in silence, with eyes piercing into my soul from every wall, I sit with my mind on Bruce. The monster the rest of the world thinks he is, I know he's only partly. Bruce isn't the pervert everyone has labeled him to be. It's true, he's significantly older than me. It's true, he played with my heart. It's true, he didn't love me as he claimed and didn't care very much about my emotional well-being. But it's also true that what happened between us, I wanted. The months of daily dialogue between the two of us, I actively participated in and encouraged. While Bruce is considered a dirty, old, gay man to most, he was a friend to me, a shoulder to lean on, a compassionate ear, a man I looked up to, a crush that was returned. He was my boyfriend. Our relationship was virtual until the one day we met, but it was still a relationship. Everyone cares about its ending. That part burdens my thoughts too, but it's not all I think about, and it doesn't erase all that he was to and for me.

A year ago, lying in bed, in the dark, I turned to a site I wouldn't advise anyone to seek friendship on. I turned to Craigslist. I never posted a picture, never described my slim, teen-age body type, never shared how dark chocolate my skin is, how acne free my face is, how pretty most people have described me to be, though I'm a guy. I simply vented. I shared details about my town, about the people, about how stuck in another century everyone is. I shared about being the son of a pastor. I detailed how awful it was to have so many of my schoolmates talk about me. I wrote about my one true friend, Nikki, and her acceptance of me. I let it all out for a world of strangers. I bled on the keys. I cried on the screen. I exposed myself as a gay teenager living in an intolerant, Godly town.

Most responses were from spammers. A few were encouraging words from other gay guys sharing their struggles and reminding me that high school is only four years of my life. Unsurprisingly, I received hate mail. You can't be gay and not be damned to hell or called a fudge packer. But one message stood out above the rest. It was from Bruce. I read his short message multiple times until I memorized every word, and I couldn't help but respond back. He wrote, *Sounds to me like your family and town are behind the times. I'm 56, gay, and there's nothing you're enduring that I haven't survived. Know what that tells me? This isn't something you can't survive. Being gay is not a phase, but what you're dealing with is. It's a short, painful, but short time, which will be a distant memory when you leave that place. After graduation, head to a big city. Meet people, other gay men, some straight too who will let you be yourself. Who knows, maybe we'll cross paths. We'll toast to your newfound freedom.* He ended the message with, *and don't forget, you don't have the problem. The intolerant assholes you're surrounded by do.* He inserted a smile using a colon and right parenthesis, and instead of signing his name, wrote, *A stranger who doesn't need to know you to love you.* My life began and ended there.

I replied, thanking him for his kind message and told him how touching it was that he had used the word *love*. I explained how empty and unloved I had felt, from waking to going to bed, as hiding who I really was had become impossible when it had seemed so easy before. I thanked him a second time, and shared that his caring message had miraculously brought a smile to my face and had given me an ounce of hope which was hard to find with so many people berating me or trying to pray me into straightness. When the rumors began traveling up and down the halls of my high school, I could escape my misery after the final bell. But when students began telling their families, and the rumors took over my town and church, I was the topic of most whispers. A schoolmate of mine was trying her damnedest to hide an obvious pregnancy. No doubt, there is premarital sex going on everywhere, regardless of how many church groups my generation is forced to be involved in. Still, my sexuality was, and still is, the one thing people can't stop thinking about, judging, and conversing about. With me around, her pregnancy seemed to be easily overlooked.

I ended the message with a third and final *thank you.* I don't recall whether or not I expected him to respond, or if I had hoped we'd build a friendship, but we had. Message exchanges were taking place daily, from morning until night, until we finally decided to talk on the phone. It didn't take long for Bruce to grow from being a distant stranger offering me needed words of encouragement, to a man offering me worldly advice, to the first man to flirt with me. Our growing flirtation and his feelings for me made him a part of my every thought. My feelings surpassed teenage lust and entered an unfamiliar territory for me. *Love*. I had fallen in love with Bruce, his bravery, his strength, his humor, his confidence, his certainty. Not only as a man, but as a gay man. I had fallen deeply for his sensitivity, his patience to be with me, and I yearned to be with him emotionally and physically.

Bruce wanted me in a way all people desire to be wanted. He loved me in a way I've witnessed other people pray to be loved. He became the love of my life, the center of my world, my future that I longed to begin.

When we finally began exchanging pictures, something he never pushed me to do or made a big deal of, we were both surprised. His attraction for me skyrocketed. He said *pretty boy* didn't do me justice. I've never looked at myself and felt pretty, but throughout middle school, girls crushed on me, the pretty boy with the baby face. My mother often shared stories of how I was often mistaken for a girl as a toddler. My father cut my hair, kept it military length, dressed me in darker colors, and stayed away from anything unisex to make my gender obvious. Still, girls found me pretty-faced. Bruce agreed, after receiving my selfie, that there was a softness to my face. He found me beautiful, a word that was never used to describe me.

He sent me his picture after going on about mine. I guess I really hadn't imagined his face, the face of a 56-year-old. I left him imageless. Faceless. His words made him real and had allowed me to find comfort in not knowing what he looked like. He was of substance. He was an ocean of feeling, an endless well of knowledge and experience that made me feel like I had a mentor, real guidance, and a new outlook on the world outside of religion and family. I felt as if he had opened me up to the idea of actual living. He gave me a new set of eyes to see the true meaning of friendship, openness, acceptance, and even marriage. I didn't need a face, a body, and now that I think about it, though I'd described myself to him, I didn't ask him for a description in return. Nothing about this was superficial for me.

I expanded his photo and ran my eyes across his tan skin and salt-and-pepper hair. Mostly salt. His eyes were squinted, barely allowing their blueness to show. His ungroomed beard and thick mustache immediately surprised me. Both were so thick and really aged him. He wore one small hoop earring, reading glasses, and laid reclined back in a lawn chair. While it's true, I'd have never taken a second look at him had I passed him in a supermarket or on the street, he was still all those things I had grown to love, appreciate, and admire. I didn't ask for a picture because I didn't care about his appearance. I cared about what he stood for and how he felt about me. So, I swallowed the teenage shallowness that tried to come out of me and decided to take him as he was. Just a regular guy, who didn't hide behind a fake photo, who lives openly and fearlessly gay.

He asked me what I thought of him, if his grey hair had scared me off and ruined the image I may have painted of him in my own mind. I didn't offer him a lengthy response, didn't reveal my initial shock. I responded with three simple words. *Nothing has changed.*

Conversations about my life, struggles, and fears seemed to dominate most of our talks, so I started listening more than yapping. I learned of Bruce's loneliness, listened quietly as he shared his coming out story. He was immediately beaten by his brother before he was thrown out of the house. His family didn't even let him stay another night. He shared tales that terrified me and others that inspired me. In a shameless voice, he confessed to briefly working as an escort to escape the brutal world of homelessness. His voice never cracked, never lowered in volume, never trailed off as he spoke about what he did to survive. He had made peace with a past he wasn't proud of, and he repeated to me that if there's anything to look forward to, it's a more tolerant, understanding world outside of my town. I believed him when he told me that his journey wasn't one I had to take.

He ended up landing a job in the post office. It paid enough for him to keep a roof over his head, and with slow steps, he was able to get on his feet. Nightlife in certain parts of his city introduced him to other gays, and after walking an uphill, bumpy road, he found his place in a homophobic world.

My confidence grew the more we conversed. Bruce was right. If he could survive being openly gay decades ago when the world was a totally different place, I could survive the rest of my senior year here until I could live freely with him. My future seemed as bright as the flags that represent my culture. But only when I was talking to him. Bruce was my pair of glasses, my sun, my smile, my next breath. I needed him. He knew that.

Making plans as an unlikely couple pulled

me out of my storm and helped me see my rainbow. Having something to look forward to with someone's hand in mine made the possibilities of anything seem endless for me. Even having a physical relationship. Like most other teenagers, it was a natural curiosity, a normal desire of mine. Though the partner of my fantasies has always had the same genitalia as me, I wanted to feel as comfortable, attractive, and as needed as anyone else would in such a personal, vulnerable experience. Bruce assured me that he would make my first, second, and fiftieth time just that. Normal, loving, pleasurable, intimate. *Perfect.*

I leave my thoughts of Bruce, focus back in on the living room where I'm sitting with eyes all around me. I push myself from the couch, leave the Bible on one of the cushions, and head for the bathroom. I undress, step inside the shower, and let the cool water cover my body until it slowly warms. Naked, alone, water pouring over me, my mind goes back to Bruce, back to someone I once needed, sometimes still believe I do, someone I often miss. Still, after all this.

I rest my forehead against the wall tiles. I shut my eyes, think back on conversations that many would expect to be awkward, but between us, never were. Bruce didn't disgust me when he described the things he wanted to do to me. He made me feel craved and dreamt of. He gave me a part of my adolescence I thought I'd have to live without, wanting someone and that someone wanting me back, wanting me even more. He made me feel like a giddy teenager. I could bear the bullshit I had to face at school every day and at church, the embarrassing questions, the dirty looks, the insults. I could take it all because I knew I would spend my free time texting and talking to Bruce. Love was always waiting for me, waiting to tuck me in every night or in the wee hours of the morning, which is when most of our conversations ended.

I remember the first time Bruce asked me to touch myself, to follow his rules as he talked me through what spending a night together would be like. I remember doing as I was told, envisioning every scene he painted in my head, moaning into the phone as his words forced feelings and even shakes out of me. I remember looking so forward to experiencing what he described and dying to meet him in person more than ever.

Though seventeen at the time, I couldn't have cared less about our differences. I wanted Bruce. Bruce wanted me. The difference in race, age, and even state didn't matter to either of us. We found a love we'd both needed. We fulfilled an emptiness in each other's lives. We were each other's smiles. Or so I thought. I can say for certain that those were my true feelings.

I breathe deeply, grab the bar of soap, pull my washcloth from the curtain rod, and lather it up. As I rub the soapy cloth against my skin, my mind travels back to what was the most special night of my life. Well, at the time it was.

Ms. Edna, one of the members of our congregation, lost her grandchild in an unfortunate accident. Because her grandchild lived in South Carolina at the time of her death, as did most of her other relatives, the services were to be held there the following weekend. My mother, father, and aunt Linda had decided to drive Ms. Edna down to support her through the funeral service and to ensure she had a safe mode of transportation to return home. After all, she's an elder and she's not sitting on millions. Over the years, her family left this unprogressive town to explore different ways of living. Outside of her church family, Ms. Edna is mostly alone. She prays and loves her relatives from a distance, leaving her to depend on those she prays with throughout the week to help her through her tough times.

I was surprised my father had offered to drive her, as his help is typically given through prayer and loud readings from the pulpit, but I was ecstatic about being left alone. Moments after signing Ms. Edna's sympathy card, I called Bruce. I told him about Ms. Edna's loss, explained that my family would be driving her to the funeral, shared how excited I was to be able to walk around my house and not be preached *at*. Not to, but at. I had always felt that my father never really spoke to me. I was never given a choice to accept what he said. He shoved every word in my face with his high volume and his deep tone.

I had explained to Bruce that I was to lead the youth group in my father's absence, but still, I was thrilled to be away from him. The gay *rumors* had already begun circulating, and my father was sure it was because my mother was so soft with me. Though he was present, he somehow thought she had made me a sissy with her nurturing ways. Nikki saved me from my father buying into what was going around. She allowed me to hide behind our platonic friendship, even walked hand in hand with me on occasion to really market what we were working overtime to sell. That didn't stop my classmates from staring at me, from commenting on my mannerisms, from listening to how I enunciated my words, from picking apart how I walked and even sat. Nikki standing in as my girlfriend didn't stop my schoolmates from keeping a vigilant watch for any slips, for any definite signs that the pastor's son was indeed a *faggot.* But our show did keep my father from calling me out of my name. Our act forced him to believe what I needed him to, and more importantly, what he needed to believe. He's our town's pastor. He can't have a gay son. He can't even have a soft son. While he bought into our false romance, he had begun criticizing how I ate, how I positioned my head for photographs, my pitch when I read from the Bible, and everything else I did in an attempt to draw attention to and help me fix what he was sure had made people question my sexuality. What was happening at school had slowly but surely begun happening at home. My schoolmates were watching for *gayness* and my father was nitpicking in an attempt to force me into manliness. Ms. Edna's loss brought me a needed gain. A break.

I waited for Bruce to tell me how happy he was for me to have a night to myself. I waited for him to excite me about the conversation we'd have throughout the night. But he didn't prepare me for a lengthy talk. He prepared me for a visit. Immediately, he told me that he wanted to see me. As we had seen it, life had thrown us an unexpected opportunity, one Bruce was anxious to take advantage of.

I never got to ask any questions. His mouth began running a mile a minute. In no time, I learned that he was going to book a flight. He was going to spend a night with me after many months of talking, finally get to hug me in person, and kiss my lips as opposed to kissing his phone receiver. He was coming to see me, look me in the eye and say *I love you.* Not once did he ask if I wanted these things. Instead, he told me what he wanted to do. Needed to do. I liked that. Loved it, actually. It felt incredibly special to hear the urgency and passion in his voice. All I could do with a heart full of joy and stomach full of flutters was say, *okay.* I didn't want to overdo it, sound too desperate, or act like a child, but inside I was over the moon. I wanted to scream. I was going to meet Bruce face to face, and I wouldn't have to pretend to be anyone or anything but who and what I really am. That made me equally petrified and thrilled. This would be the first time I'd be able to be unhidden in front of another man. Another gay man.

When our night had arrived, I had to take multiple showers after my parents left. Stress sweat was pouring out of me like blood from an open wound. When Bruce had finally got to my house, I was fresh out of the shower and dressed in slacks and a button down. It was late, already dark out, and my parents had already made their goodnight call.

Bruce was dropped at the end of my street and walked to my door. He had traveled light, carried only one bag slung across his body. He never knocked. He didn't need to. I saw him walk up. With a pounding heart and a jittering hand, I quickly pulled the door open to let him enter before any of my nosy neighbors could see him. He stepped in, and I rushed to close and lock the door. Alone, in my home, Bruce and I stood before one another. My entire body trembled. He was in front of me. We were to ourselves. Just me and Bruce. Me and my boyfriend.

He pulled the strap from around him and let his bag fall to the floor. Hurriedly, he moved toward me. He pulled my body to his and held me close. He whispered one word to me as we hugged, one word that summed up how we both felt. *Finally.*

He could feel my body shaking and found a variety of ways to tell me to relax and that I'd be okay. He took my hand and, after picking his bag up, followed me through my dark house to my bedroom. I wanted the lights off to indicate to my neighbors that I'd tucked myself in for the night, just in case they were keeping tabs for my father. In my room, my door shut, our only light a Febreze candle, Bruce and I sat on the floor. My back rested against my bed and his against my door which made me feel protected. Together for the first time, we looked at each other. No phones between us. No distance.

"It's good to finally see you," he said. "You look even better in person."

I lowered my head and thanked him without looking him in the eye.

"Am I too ugly to look at for more than a few seconds? Too old?"

Immediately, I made eye contact. "No."

He chuckled lightly. "Just a little icebreaker."

"You look the same," I told him. "I just can't believe you're here, that we're together."

"That's all we talk about, Jo."

Jo. He'd begun calling me that early in our conversations and I never stopped him. Aside from Bruce, Nikki was and still is the only person to call me by a nickname. My father would never allow such a thing. Shortening such a powerful name, a name found in the Bible, a name carried by Jesus's earthly father would earn me a hit, a smack right to the face. But I liked and still do like nicknames. They're casual, personal, and make me feel like I have a real connection with someone. Being called something other than Joseph by Bruce made me feel closer to him, like our relationship really was intimate. Intimate and real.

With my washcloth still in hand, warm water continues to cover my body as my mind replays the night I spent with Bruce. His face is framed in my mind. A still shot of him from our night.

I had replied to his statement. "It's all we talk about, but it was a plan that could've never happened."

"But it did happen," he said. "I'm here. I told you I was going to come see you whenever I could if it wouldn't get you into trouble. I told you we would be together. I told you I'm a man of my word. I love you, Jo."

My eyes had remained on his as he said those words to me in person. I said it back without letting my eyes leave his.

"This is a pretty nice house for a town that's mentally stuck in another century," he said, scanning my room as he sat. "I expected creaky, wood floors, plaid bedding, murals of the last supper."

"You just described the inside of most of the other houses around here, though we all have framed images of the last supper. I told you before, my father moves with the times in some ways. I mean, we do have cell phones, and he's remodeled this place a few times. I sent you pictures of the new deck, remember? He just doesn't think any differently than his father did. Their way of thinking is the only way, and it's been passed down for many generations and isn't expected to stop at mine."

"So, after you move in with me, you're cutting them off completely?" he asked.

"I'd hate to think that I'd never see or talk to my mother again, but if my father learns that I have no intention of following in his footsteps and taking over the church, he's going to snap and then disown me. By default, my mother would, too."

"So, it'd just be you and me. No baggage," Bruce said.

"No baggage? I'm carrying a ton of emotional baggage."

"We're all carrying emotional baggage. The good thing about us is I've mostly dealt with mine, so there's nothing hindering me from helping you sort through and overcome yours."

I offered Bruce a half smile. I loved being with him, but hated that our visit would have to be so short. He'd have to go at the crack of dawn. He'd have to leave before any neighbors could see him step outside of my house.

Bruce pulled a bottle from his bag. I'd never drunk anything stronger than the grape juice served at communion, but with him, I had champagne. I remember standing to go grab cups, but he insisted we relax. Back and forth we passed the bottle, taking sips. My mind thought less and less about how short our visit would be and simply allowed me to just enjoy it. I laughed a lot. I remember that. I can't say for certain if Bruce's statements were as funny as I had made them seem, but I was having the best time I'd ever had listening to him talk about his various experiences and relationships over the years. Somehow, we had ended up on the topic of career goals and dreams. I remember Bruce begging me to stay focused, begging me to relentlessly pursue whatever my heart desired. I had shared with him my dreams of wanting to go to college, my dreams of pursuing marine biology or another degree that would allow me to spend my days with animals. I'd never been able to share that with anyone other than Nikki. My dreams were made for me the moment I was born to my father. I was to become a pastor, marry a God-loving woman, and have children—hopefully, a son that would carry on our family's tradition.

I had told Bruce that I wanted to carry on a personal relationship with God without attending church amongst those who felt that all gays should and would undoubtedly burn in Hell. He had told me that in the real world, in the wide world outside of the little one I currently live in, there are churches that open their doors to all, and pastors who leave the judging to God. I told him that I looked forward to experiencing that, to living a life where I could make choices for myself. Good or bad.

Bruce asked me, "What kind of choices will you be making tonight?"

My belly sank. I took another sip from the bottle, followed by a deep breath. I wanted to start making my own choices right away. Right then and there. I didn't want to wait until moving out. I didn't want to wait months until I turned eighteen. I wanted my first time. I didn't know if it was a good or bad choice, a smart or naïve one, if it was the champagne clouding my thoughts or if it was actually me, but I looked him in the eye and had silently ended the wait. Bruce had made the same decision. He opened his bag to show me he had come prepared for the same thing.

That night, we kissed, we touched, did all I had looked forward to doing with him. He gave instructions. I followed them. He asked. He received. I felt things I never thought I'd feel, did things I never thought I'd feel comfortable enough to do, and fell deeper than I'd thought possible. He was mine. Really mine. My one and only love. And I was his. Or so I thought.

Early the next morning, before daybreak, I was awakened by sounds of him dressing and throwing evidence of our night back into his bag. Naked, I remained under my blanket. I watched quietly for a few minutes before alerting him to the fact that I was awake. Though the room was dark, I could see him slowly moving about. My heart was splitting slowly as I knew he had to leave me. We had only had hours together, and already I had to say goodbye. He had to go before anyone could witness him leaving. He had to walk away from me after making love to me for the first time.

In only boxers, I walked with him to the door. Tears desperately wanted to rush from my eyes. My heart hurt so badly, I was sure I was going to die from its breaking, but I kept quiet, held in the emotion, fought to find the perfect words to not say goodbye, but see you later. I wanted to say something meaningful, to find words that could really let him know how he had made me feel, but I couldn't.

At the door, we stood silently. His bag was slung over his shoulder the way it was when he had arrived. He stared at me, never parting his lips. Neither of us spoke, cried, or shared what was in our hearts. He unlocked the door, and before walking out, placed his hand on my cheek, brought my face closer to his, and kissed me softly. His kiss said I love you, I'll miss you, and I'll never forget our night. His silent exit screamed of a pain like what I was feeling.

In hindsight, I wish I'd thought about how Bruce had even found my ad. We don't and never did live in the same state. I wish I had questioned his sincerity more. I wish I had asked why he chose my ad. I wish I could've seen through my love haze. I wish I could've seen it coming, could've at least prepared myself slightly with just silent, internal questions of *what if.*

I never saw it coming, never thought after coming out of the closet to my father that Bruce wouldn't care to hear me talk about it. I never thought for even a second that I would be nothing more than a new piece of ass for him, just a new notch in his belt. Not when he was everything and more to me.

Never did I think my night of firsts would also be my night of lasts. *Never.* I most definitely never thought the day when I'd finally get to meet him would also be the day he'd leave me.

CHAPTER 3

I sit on the bed, facing the true love of my life. The one who has never questioned me. The one who has loved me through it all. My best friend. My real soulmate. My Nikki.

"You smell nice, JJ."

"Fresh out the shower."

"You're wearing cologne, too."

I shrug. "It's the one you bought me for my birthday. I don't really wear cologne, but I figured, why not today?"

She smiles, revealing teeth braces took two years to perfect. "Just for me."

"Anything for you," I tell her right away.

"You always say that."

"I mean it. You have no idea how much having you has meant to me throughout this whole thing."

"I'm not going anywhere, JJ. Ever."

I look at my friend's beautiful face. I touch her thick, coarse hair. It isn't straightened today.

Her bush is wild and untamed.

"What are you staring at?"

"You're flawless, Nikki."

She rolls her eyes. "Boy, bye."

"Really, Nik. You may have more body than most eighteen-year-olds, but it's a work of art. You're a chocolate goddess. Everyone can see that. So why am I not attracted to you? Why don't I want you?"

She takes my hand. "Because you're gay, and regardless of what we've been taught, I don't think there's anything wrong with you. We come from the same God, right?"

"Right," I answer softly.

"So, there can't be anything wrong with you. Not if the same perfect God that made your father, me, and everyone else made you, too. You're just gay, JJ. You're not a child molester, a killer, or a sadist. You just like guys. Shit, there are worse things than being gay. I just wish they'd leave you the fuck alone. Who are you hurting?"

I don't answer.

"No one!" she answers for me. "Not a damn soul. We're just stuck in a town full of judgmental assholes who hide behind a book they clearly didn't read thoroughly. If they did, they wouldn't judge you or treat you the way they do. That's against everything we're taught. You just need to get out of here. We both do. We need to settle in a city, live like normal people, and live in the 21st century with the rest of the world."

"There are judgmental people everywhere, Nikki."

"Yeah, but most of them keep their damn mouths closed because discrimination isn't a worldwide, expectable thing. I'm not saying you won't face any more challenges or hear another hurtful slur. I'm saying you'll be around more people who accept you or have been taught to live beside you no matter how they live or what they believe in."

I nod. I want that. I want that so much. I want to live openly, freely, fearlessly, but I can't. No matter where I go, I'm still going to face discrimination of some sort. People aren't wearing *Black Lives Matter* t-shirts for no reason. My color still isn't universally accepted. To complicate my life even further, I'm gay. In the black community, especially in the eyes of other black men, being homosexual is the worst thing you can be. You can sell drugs to minors and be forgiven, hit your wife and be given a second chance, even take a life and receive understanding. But when it comes to homosexuality, when it comes to gay men, far too many people tend to overlook the love that can and often does exist. They just can't seem to focus on anything other than the sex, the private encounters that happen behind closed doors. That's disappointing. Considering all that's wrong in this world, all the major issues that need focus, I can't believe anyone would wrap themselves in legal, personal matters that have nothing to do with them. Of all the things to judge and obsess about, I can't believe gay couples are on anyone's mind.

"Wouldn't you like to be my roommate?" she asks.

"Of course. Best friends living together in a new city. That'd be great. Only, a trial begins tomorrow. That trial is centered around me. I can't dream right now, Nikki. My dreams were blown to bits the moment that bullet blew through my chest."

"No they weren't because you're still here. Your dreams are still here, too. You're just distracted from them, JJ. That coward didn't take your dreams any more than he took your life. He wounded you. That's it. You being here is proof that your purpose still hasn't been served."

"And what's my purpose?"

"To help animals. You're supposed to be a marine biologist. You're supposed to do your part to keep animals of all kinds from becoming extinct. And you're supposed to have a family. Some unwanted child out there is waiting for you to take them in and show them the love your father doesn't know how to show you. And you're supposed to be a lifelong best friend to me. You teach me strength whether you know that or not. You bring something into my life that no other friend or even family member has been able to. And for that, I'll always love you."

My stomach tightens as a sharpness stabs at my heart. Hearing how much I mean to Nikki is as beautiful as it is painful. I wish her love, her platonic but sincere love, were enough to get me through this year. I wish it had kept me off the internet. Though I thought Bruce was someone I had needed, though I thought he was someone he wasn't, I've never been unsure about Nikki. No matter what she hears or reads, she never stops being a true friend. She's never ashamed or embarrassed to walk beside me. She never stops defending me.

"I love you too, Nik."

I move to sit beside her. I glide my pointer across the softness of the back of her hand. I touch her fingers, something I've always found comfort in doing, something she's never pulled away from.

"How do you feel about tomorrow?" she asks, her voice so low, so gentle. "Anxious? Terrified?"

I shrug. I don't know how to accurately describe how I feel because my feelings are ever-changing and so unstable. I know it's up to me to iron out the oh-so-many wrinkles in this case. I know I have to be the one to reveal surprising truths, but still, I don't know what I really feel about what's to come or how to describe my burden.

I say, "I don't know. The most annoying part of all this is the media. They don't know everything, so they fill in the blanks with read-worthy drama. It sells magazines, earns clicks, and makes millions watch the news, but it affects people. People like me. I was already the victim of attempted murder and then the media re-victimized me repeatedly. Some outlets even claimed I was selling myself online. That's a complete lie, a seed they planted that grew into other lies. I just needed to vent. I never thought one Craigslist posting would lead me here."

She grips my hand. "Everything happens for a reason, JJ. This is your storm. It sounds corny, but brighter days will come. After the trial."

I shake my head. I'm so tired of hearing about life after the trial. I'm so tired of hearing about future relief. I'm so tired of hearing and even thinking about what happened.

I close my eyes, put myself in darkness. Through the darkness peers moonlight. Enough for me to see the gun, the barrel, his finger on the trigger. Our eyes make direct contact as the gun fires. The sound of the gunshot echoes in my ear. Blood mists all over my pillow as I turn over. Short, jagged, rapid breaths make it impossible to call out for help, to take a full breath. I'm dying, can feel my life leaving me, as he leaves out my window with the gun in hand. I cough, watch more blood spray out of my mouth, cry because he saw me see him. He knows I love him, knows I'd never hurt him, and he took the shot anyway. He looked me in the eye and pulled the trigger. He put a hole in my chest.

My eyes spring back open. I feel a heaviness in my chest like a brick wall is being pushed into me. I pull my hand from Nikki's, touch where the pain is, rub it in a panic, encourage diaphragmatic breathing, repeat calming phrases to myself that Dr. Benson has taught me. My breathing doesn't even out. It becomes more sporadic, more painful, more of a struggle.

Nikki gasps. "JJ! Oh God! What do you need? Should I call an ambulance? Do you need your medicine?"

I shake my head, continue to release breaths I can't get control of.

"You're scaring me, JJ. I think I should call someone."

"I'm... I'm..." I shut my eyes tightly. *Calm breaths, Joseph. Take calm, deep breaths.*

Self-coaching fails me. It feels like the weight of the world is on me, sitting right on my chest, pressing the life out of my heart. Even Nikki's words of encouragement are too much to bear. Everything said to me, every look I receive takes me back to what happened. I can't escape it. This town isn't the only place I need out of. I need out of my own mind too.

Nikki positions herself in front of me, pushes my hand away, and places her hand over my heart. I look down at her hand, a hand I can't feel. All I feel is pressure, pressure from the entire world, and it hurts. It's suffocating.

"Stay with me." She inhales deeply and exhales slowly. "Come on, JJ. Breathe with me. Hang onto my voice. Stay with me."

My hands begin shaking uncontrollably.

The echo of the shot rings in my ear, making her voice mute. I take my quivering hand and place it on top of hers. I want to feel her. I need to. I need to feel my friend, her support, something real and right in my fucked-up world. But I can't. Her softness, her love, her sincerity can't break through all the torture I've been forced to endure. Torture that's turned into a never-ending cycle of daymares and nightmares. Torture that's become a thick, hard wall that hope and kindness are no longer strong enough to break through. And this wall was slowly built. One insult wasn't strong enough for it to take full form, to rob me of feeling like an actual being. Countless insults, threats, and being handed eternal sentences to Hell from everyone around me on a daily basis is what it took for them to slowly, but callously and remorselessly build this inside me. I can't break through it to even feel real anymore. As much as I'm tired of thinking about what happened, I can't stop. As far as a future goes, I can't see past a trial that will in no way serve justice. Together, they robbed me of whatever real life I was supposed to have.

Their cruel words have sliced into my heart and become embedded in my memory. Their stares filled with intimidation and disgust have created an irreversible fear of looking others in the eye. Bruce's abandonment didn't leave me feeling empty. It left me alone to question everything about myself, to feel completely used and unlovable. That gunshot has become a part of my mental playlist, and I can't seem to remove it from my memory for even a day.

I see Nikki's lips moving, but I can't hear anything but the echo of the shot. Her hand is still on me, but I still feel the pain. A pain *they* think I deserve to feel because I'm gay.

She stops talking, goes back to demonstrating deep breathing. I fight with myself to stop shaking. I keep my eyes on the most beautiful person I've ever had in my life, the person I'm convinced is the most beautiful in this town, in this whole world. I blink a few times, but don't allow my eyes to stay shut for too long. I don't want to see it all again.

She takes a deep breath. I do the same.

"Keep going. You're doing great, JJ. Give me another one."

I can hear her again. *Thank God.* I keep my eyes on hers and do as she's asked. I inhale deeply and exhale as slowly as I can. "Keep... Keep talking to me," I say. "Please. I need to hear your voice."

She takes her other hand and wipes sweat from my forehead. "We shouldn't be here. We should be where you feel safest. We'll talk there."

I nod, let a tear fall because her level of understanding surpasses that of a normal friend. She's undeniably my soulmate, the single greatest part of my entire existence.

She takes my hands in hers. On quaking legs that feel like jelly, I somehow manage to take the few short steps. In the small space, we sit face to face. In my space, absent of a window, I hold hands with Nikki. Beneath my hung clothing, we sit cross-legged and eye one another.

"Would you like some water? I could grab you some."

I shake my head. "Don't leave. I'm fine. This is what I needed. You and this closet."

"This closet isn't the only one you need. I wish you could've stayed in the other closet too."

I squeeze her hand.

"Not because I think you should have to hide, but because it served as your protection in this town. I hate him for that," she says, shaking her head. "I hate that he promised you a future, safety, love, and then let you fall all by yourself. I feel like he pushed you out of a plane with a defective chute."

"I wish he hadn't played with my emotions like that either. I feel more crushed about that than being used for sex. More than a physical relationship, I needed acceptance. Real…"

"I've always accepted you," she interrupts. "Before you even accepted yourself, I accepted you."

"I know. But I needed that acceptance from a man, too."

She nods. She doesn't have to tell me she understands. I know she does.

I shrug. "Well, I thought I did."

"I can understand why you'd need that. This town is small compared to the rest of the world, but it's where you live. It's all you know. Everyone knows everyone. Everyone thinks the same way. Being the minority, well in your case, the only, must feel incredibly lonely. Though you have me, we'd never be more than best friends. You needed someone like you. I get that. You could relate to him differently and be a different kind of open with him. I just wish he was who he typed and talked himself up to be. Even if it didn't end up working out for you two, I still wish he hadn't come into your life just to use you and break your heart."

I shrug. "I wish that too, but what's done is done."

"Do you still think about him?" Her voice becomes a whisper. "I'm not talking about the night I almost lost you. I'm talking about before that happened."

I nod.

She forces a half smile.

"Do you think I'm stupid for thinking about him, for sometimes believing I may actually miss him? You know, the him he painted himself to be."

"Hell no, I don't think you're stupid. I wasn't thrilled that you didn't tell me about him right away or that he was 56 years old, but what he did for you was something I couldn't. How could you not miss him?"

My hands twitch at the thought of who I once believed to be my everything.

"Look, JJ," she says, her hands still in mine. "I get it. And as a friend, shit, as a human, I won't ask, nor do I expect you to forget him. But as a friend, I do want you to look forward to the real thing. Look forward to dating someone in person, not on the computer or on your phone. Look forward to meeting someone closer to your age, who picks you once they lay eyes on you and vice versa. Look forward to experiencing gay pride. Look forward to life. Look forward to all those things he used to talk to you about but look forward to them with someone you'll meet and actually grow into experiencing those things with. Bruce found you by trolling through ads for dejected young men. You didn't find him. Out in the real world, outside of this closed-minded, time forgotten little town, people find each other."

"Is that why you haven't asked about what went down with us? Because you think of him as some creep, trolling through ads for crying, teenage boys?"

She shrugs. "I didn't ask because I thought it'd make you uncomfortable. You didn't tell me anything that happened between you and Bruce right after it happened. You were talking to him for months before you had even told me about posting on Craigslist. You didn't tell me that he came by until months after it happened, and things were already on the rocks with you two. I didn't want to make it worse by asking for details of a night I figured you'd share with me if you wanted me to know."

I lower my head and stare at the floor. "Sometimes I want to talk about it with you."

"But?"

I shrug, never lifting my head. "I get freaked out wondering what kind of response you'll give me to the details."

"Well, wait until you're not so freaked out. I'm in no rush. You'll tell me everything you want me to know when you feel ready."

"You're so understanding and considerate of everything. I know you'd never act like a drama queen, but still, it's not heterosexual sex we'd be talking about. It's not the story of two teenagers."

"I do know what kind of sex gay men have, JJ."

"But I'd be telling you about me. Not some random story I read about someone else."

"You know what I think? I think your father being a pastor, your expectations as his son, and the response from this community has forced you to believe that what you did was wrong. I'm sure you didn't do anything with Bruce I didn't think you'd eventually do anyway. And I also think you're embarrassed to talk about it because it was a first for you and you have doubts about yourself because Bruce did a 180 afterward. The thing is, what Bruce did was foul. The guy is a sick, fucking asshole. Worse than that actually, but you get my point. Still, what you did with him, I'm sure you'll do in your future relationships, too. Unless, you're keeping some creepy, dark secrets." Her face scrunches.

My stomach sinks. "Like what? What would be considered creepy?"

"Bruce wasn't one of those weird internet guys who liked to stick rats or possums up his ass, was he?"

Laughter surprisingly flies out of me. I don't know when I last heard myself laugh.

She laughs too. "Was he?"

"No, Nikki!"

"Did he ask you to take a dump on his chest?"

"Eww. No."

"Then I'm sure whatever you did won't make me pull my friend card."

We both laugh, and it sounds so beautiful. It sounds nice to hear real laughter because of a joke, to see eyes tear up due to cracking up and not because of what happened to me.

"It's so good to hear you laugh. I think I forgot what that sounded like."

I smile at Nikki. "Me too."

"I miss times like this. Times when we're not forced to sit in church and act like little angels, but can just hang out alone, talk, and be teenage dirtbags."

I nod. "Me too."

She smiles. "Remember when we finally got some balls and watched that video *Two Girls*

One Cup?"

I cringe. "That was the most disgusting thing I had ever seen, and I don't think we watched a full minute."

"Actually, I think we saw the trailer. I can't remember. It's old, but I saw a reaction video on Facebook and had to see what all the fuss was about. Couldn't do it without you."

"Since then, I've been hesitant about saying *okay* to the things you want to show me."

She chuckles. "I'm hesitant about clicking on random links or looking up what others are talking about on social media. I seriously almost vomited seeing just a clip of that. But still, we've never stopped laughing about it."

"That's true. Your secret social media accounts have been our source of comedy and viral filth." I caress her cheek. "And that's why being with you beats being with anyone else. You make me feel normal. You're my touch to the real world. I thought Bruce was, but it's you. It's always been you."

She touches my cheek. "You are normal. I make you feel like what you are. What's not normal is where we live. You have to keep reminding yourself of that."

I sigh, pull her hand from my face, and hold it tightly in mine. "I want to tell you about it.

About my night with Bruce. I want to look you in the eye and tell you what we did, and I want you to use your Nikki magic and make it feel normal. My mind and my heart go back and forth. It was a special night for me, but after the police got a hold of my emails and leaked information to the media, the world started commenting on how he became uninterested in me afterward and how I began chasing him, trying to make him love me. They publicized how he had abandoned me after sex and after I'd come out to my family. They had a field day talking about how I emailed him and texted him repeatedly, virtually crying and begging him for support and responses. They paraphrased his replies, his demands for me go away. It felt like they were laughing about the fact that he had threatened me, and not too soon after, I ended up shot. They called him a perverted, stupid criminal for leaving a paper trail."

"I know. I read that somewhere."

"They made everything about us dirty, forbidden, sick. But this is my life, and in a lot of ways, they got it so wrong, Nikki. They dug so far into Bruce and me, and their opinions took over so much, I started to question how I felt about what was once special. He devastated me afterward, but that night wasn't what they say."

"Tell me about it."

I swallow and exhale. "It was something I was looking forward to, but I was so nervous about it. I kept sweating in anticipation of his arrival."

"Were you worried about how you'd look to him or how he'd look in person?"

"I was just nervous in general. It was a first for everything. He was my first boyfriend. That was our first time meeting, our first night being alone, my first time drinking."

Her eyes widen. "You drank?"

"He brought champagne with him."

"Liquid courage. He came prepared. Did you like it?"

"It was okay. It loosened me up. Made the evening feel romantic and grown up."

"I bet. Can't wait until I finally get to sip some bubbly."

"It'll definitely make you feel warm and less guarded. It made me less nervous while we talked."

"About sex?"

"No. About life. He told me about his past dating disasters, and I couldn't stop laughing. I told him about my dreams, my love for animals, and he repeated to me how important it was for me to pursue my passions. We talked about everything. It was funny, but comforting to talk about life in person. It would've been so awkward to meet, and sex be all he wanted to discuss."

"I'm glad he didn't show up acting like a horndog. Did he look better in person?"

"The same."

"Is he your type?"

"I don't think I have a type. With Bruce, I fell in love with everything he stood for, said, and how he made me feel. When I looked at him, I saw what he embodied, not the difference in our age."

"I get that. But did you find him physically attractive? Truthfully?"

I look down before shaking my head.

"So, you lost your virginity to someone you weren't attracted to?"

"But I was attracted to him—to who he was."

"I'm sure you were, but if you had other options, other guys chatting you up, he wouldn't have been who you chose."

"Still, I chose him."

"No, JJ. He chose you."

"Well, he didn't force me."

"I know, and I'm not trying to make you feel worse. I'm not trying to sound like everybody else. I just want you to remember that you're safe with me. You can say the uncomfortable stuff. I won't laugh, and I won't pick now to start judging you. Just say it. Tell the truth, JJ. It won't make you anything but normal. People sleep with people they're not attracted to all the time. Many teens lose their virginity and wish they could go back and experience it differently or with someone else. It's not uncommon. It's called regret. We all regret something. You may have enjoyed some of the night, but lay it all out for me. If something was off, you can finally say so. If something was amazing, you can finally brag. All I want is for you to be able to freely and honestly share it with me."

I exhale. I'm finally being given the opportunity to share the truth of a night I've kept to myself. I haven't even been able to revisit it with Bruce, to share my feelings about it with him because he lost interest in talking to me after using my body. Now I can let it out, share what was amazing, what was uncomfortable, what was painful, everything. As always, I can count on Nikki. My rock.

"Start over, JJ, and give me nothing but the truth. No matter how embarrassing, I'm all ears, and my support fully belongs to you."

I make eye contact, nod, prepare to talk

about something she's already made me feel better about. I've spent so much time trying to understand why I was abandoned, so much time in my head feeling bad because I can't defend Bruce against the outright lies people have fabricated about him, so much time focusing on what was almost the last night of my life, I haven't been truthful with myself about how things really were. I loved Bruce, looked forward to a life with him, wanted sex with him, but my fantasies weren't perfect and weren't totally romantic because I wasn't physically attracted to him. However, Bruce was my only option, or at least it seemed that way. From message one, he expressed nothing but kindness and love. How could I complain? He brought so much into my hopeless, grim world and I was grateful and moved by him. After all, if one is trapped in the dark with only a tea candle, they're not likely to complain that the flame is too small. They're simply going to appreciate their only source of light. That's why I appreciated Bruce so much. In my small, closed-off, hateful world, he was my only source of male guidance, future stability, male acceptance, and romantic love. He was my light. My much-needed light.

"I didn't find him attractive," I say. "When

I saw his photo, I was a bit surprised because I had never pictured him. His words painted such an amazing person, I didn't need to create any physical images. When we exchanged pictures, only one of us was sincerely over the moon about what they saw. He constantly complimented my looks."

"While you may have hidden your true feelings, and made him believe you found him attractive, I don't think he was working to convince you. I believe the physical attraction was there for him, JJ. Please don't ever convince yourself that you're not attractive. You are so easy to look at," she tells me. "I just wanted to say that. Keep going."

"It's weird because as much as I didn't find him hot, I wanted to be with him. I needed my first time to be with Bruce."

She nods.

"So we talked, we drank, shared laughs, and got comfortable in front of one another. While being with him, I had decided I wanted to take things to the next level. I chose." I point to myself. "He came prepared, but it was me, Nikki. I made the choice. I wanted him as much as he wanted me."

She nods again. "I'm sure. You guys became close after all those months of daily talk and fantasizing."

I swallow and take a deep breath. "He kissed me."

"Your first kiss. How was it?"

I shrug. "Wasn't bad, but I was a shaky mess. Even with the champagne in me, even though I wanted it, the physical contact brought on nerves that my tipsiness couldn't block me from feeling. And I wasn't even sure that I was doing it right."

"I understand that. It was your first time, and he was more experienced than you."

"He didn't complain about me, though. We ended up kissing a lot, so I think I ended up liking it. I felt more comfortable with each kiss and definitely fell more in love."

She offers me a smile, a comforting push for me to keep talking.

My hand twitches as I think about Bruce taking it in his hand, guiding it to where he wanted it. "Then he put my hand on his..." I pause, try to think of how to word this. I want to be open with Nikki, but I don't want to be too descriptive. I don't want to disgust her. Most people can take hearing about sex, but this was sex between two men.

"Hey," she calls out, grabbing my hand. "Get out your head. Stop thinking of filters. Stop worrying about what you think my reaction is going to be. Stop forgetting that I'm your best friend. There's no judgment here, JJ. Say it. He put your hand on his penis, his cock, his dick, his meat stick?"

"Okay, Nikki."

"No, it's not okay. It's not okay that you've been criticized so much, you're scared of talking freely behind closed doors with your friend. Your ace. You can call it whatever you want. You can be as descriptive as you want to be. I just thought I'd fully break the ice for you by showing you how dirty you can talk if you choose to. No matter what you say or what you tell me you did, I'm not going to run out of here puking."

I stare at my friend, admire her flawless face, which is as beautiful as her open heart is. Everyone needs a Nikki in their life, and I'm more than blessed to have her. "I'll stick with the word penis," I say.

"Fine. Penis it is."

I say softly, "Thank you, Nikki."

"For?"

"This. For not just opening the door, but for opening it up and allowing me to walk through it with any and everything."

"That's what I'm here for. You already started. Keep going. Walk on through."

My hand twitches again. "So, like I was saying, he put my hand on his penis. First, he had me rubbing it over his pants, but then he took his hand away and asked me for skin to skin contact. I couldn't go in his pants on my own, so he guided me again and helped me out. You know, showing me what to do, and how he liked to be touched. He controlled the movements of my hand and then eventually took his away, and I stroked him on my own."

"Did you like it?

"I liked how he reacted to my touch."

"Did he touch you back?"

"He unbuttoned my shirt while I stroked him, and he continued to kiss me. Then he touched my face and rubbed his hand across my hair. As soon as he did that, I knew what he wanted. We had talked about it, but doing is always different."

"Always," she agrees.

"So, he asked. He asked if I could bring our conversations to life. He asked if he could feel my lips where he had fantasized about feeling them."

She watches me as I speak, never cringes, never expresses any revulsion.

"And I did it. He asked, and I gave." Before

Nikki can ask if I enjoyed it, I say, "It wasn't horrible. I wasn't sure that I'd be comfortable enough to do that for him, but I did it, and he loved it. And because he loved it, I didn't mind it. I wanted to make him happy."

"And what did he do to make you happy?"

"That really did make me happy, Nikki. Giving. Pleasing. Selfless acts for someone else. Isn't that love? I enjoyed showing him how much I loved him. It actually made me feel closer to him. It made me fall deeper for him."

"So, what selfless acts did he perform for you? What did he do to prove his love to you?"

"He showed up for me. He listened to me. He didn't judge me or belittle me. He made me feel wanted, needed, important."

Nikki looks away from me.

"What? Say what's on your mind."

"I love you, JJ, so I'm not going to lie to you. The sexual details aren't bothering me. It's how you're processing this that's upsetting me. I get that it wasn't the disgusting, sick experience everyone else thinks it was. He didn't come to your house and rape you. He didn't push you to do things you were dead set against. But he did use you. He showed up prepared to take your virginity. Sex can either seal something for a man or start something new for the relationship.

It was you who told me that years ago when I first started getting so much attention, and I still think of your words whenever I get any type of sexual thought. You have to remember your own words now. In this case, sadly, he only wanted to seal the deal."

My head drops, my stomach churns, my hands shake. A heat wave slowly moves across my body. I feel hot. Sick. I feel like I may vomit, but I really just want to pass out. I want to escape this pain, to not feel it anymore.

"You may have felt that showing up was enough, but he didn't show up because he loved you. He showed up to take advantage of someone whose heart he held in his pocket. He browsed Craigslist ads in his area, and in neighboring states, looking for lost young men he could woo and have sex with. He's not a rapist. He's not targeting prepubescent boys. He's not hiding behind fake photos. I get all that. But he's still a predator, JJ. He preys on those who are alone, in the closet, and insecure. He takes his time, gets to know them, earns their trust, wins them over emotionally, meets up with them, has sex with them, and then abandons them. And he sounds like a fucking expert at what he does, like he's had plenty of experience meeting guys online and destroying them."

My entire body shakes as I listen to truths I don't allow myself to even think. I've convinced myself that my experience was something it wasn't. It wasn't what others say, but it's not the lies I've convinced myself of either. Bruce was kind to me, I did enjoy kissing him, and I did find joy in pleasing him. That's the truth. But there's a truth I hide from, and it's that I didn't enjoy the sex at all. Many virgins don't enjoy their first time because of the discomfort, but there's usually a second time that feels better, continued communication that comforts them afterward. All I have is that one night, and he enjoyed it entirely. I didn't. I enjoyed our talk, intimately kissing Bruce, drinking for the first time, and showing Bruce how much I loved him. I didn't enjoy the painful feeling of having him inside my body, and I hated having to watch him leave me. There were no comforting talks, no promises for a better next time. Just lonely nights, lying in bed alone staring at my phone screen, impatiently waiting for his texts and calls that never arrived.

"Damn him! I've convinced myself of fucking lies just so my every thought wouldn't be painful, but you're right. He chose me because my ad screamed desperation. I believed a stranger. I let him inside my heart, inside my body, Nikki. He promised me he wouldn't hurt me. He swore he loved me. He lied about everything just so he could fuck me. My first experience was nothing to him and everything to me. I feel so dumb!"

Nikki wraps her arms around me, holds me firmly, cries with me.

Still shaking with the uncomfortable, raw truth pouring from my eyes, I say, "It hurt, Nikki. I knew it wasn't going to be amazing because it was my first time, but it really hurt. Still through all the pain, hearing him moaning made it worth it. I cared more about him and what he felt than I did myself. I really loved Bruce. I loved him more than I can describe. His 56-year-old face wasn't enough to kill my feelings. Though that experience wasn't everything I thought it'd be, when he left, I was still hopeful, and I was way more in love. What the fuck is wrong with me, Nikki? How could I have found that special?"

She squeezes my shaking body tighter and sniffles. "Nothing. Not a damn thing is wrong with you. You simply met the wrong man, and he took advantage of your vulnerability."

My stomach twists. My heart drums out a devastating beat. Tears continue to build as fast as they fall, blurring my vision. I shut my eyes.

Immediately, the gun goes off, forcing me to jolt, to cringe, as the echo repeats in my ear. My eyes pop back open, and I cling to my friend. I beg her to talk to me, to say anything, to keep me with her and out of my own mind.

"I'm right here. It's just us, JJ. Just me and you."

Eyes open, filled with tears, and I see Bruce. It's just Nikki and me in this closet, but he's still a part of me. Bruce will never leave me. That's a thought I once warmly wrapped myself in, but today it's a reality I die a little knowing. I want him to leave my memory entirely, but that'll never happen.

"I love you, JJ. I'm here."

Nikki scoots back and rests her back against the wall. She pulls my head to her legs, and like a child, I turn to my side and curl into the fetal position. My head rests on her thighs as she gently caresses my face.

Tears continue to run from my eyes and fall onto her legs. I want to close my eyes, but I don't want to see anything, to hear the *pop.* I want to rest, but my body isn't tired enough to force sleep on me. Easing into sleep doesn't consist of a few yawns followed by peaceful rest. It's a traumatic experience. What I see and hear behind my eyelids aren't nightmares. They're my realities played again and again for me to hear and see, even taste. I see the gun. I hear it fire. I can smell and even taste my own blood. I can't escape it, and beginning tomorrow morning, I'll have to sit amongst those who have played the worst roles in my life and listen to them detail what they think happened to me. I'll have to sit quietly and listen to people argue about my tragedy, rip apart my relationship with Bruce, and fire insults at my sexuality which they'll conclude is my choice. My want.

"I still think I should come to court with you. You're going to need a friend there. Someone who's really on your side."

I don't respond to Nikki. Telling her not to show up isn't something I need to repeat.

"You shouldn't have to sit in the same room with the man who shot you without someone there to hold your hand, JJ. Though I'd have to sit behind you, you'd have someone there who truly loves you. You're going to have to sit feet away from the man who put a hole in your chest, who aimed to put a hole in your heart. Do you know how hard that's going to be for you? You're going to walk into that courtroom and be overcome with emotion. Fear. Shock. Anger. Sadness. And no one will be there to remind you that you're not alone. No one will be there to whisper that they love you. You'll need me," she says, her voice cracking. "Seeing Bruce tomorrow will probably send you into a full-blown panic attack, especially since he's there to deny everything he did. You could even pass out, JJ. The last time you saw him, he was standing over you with a gun in his hand. You're not going to be in the courtroom with your ex who broke your heart. You're going to be in the courtroom with true evil, with the gunman."

Aunt Linda is sure that seeing Bruce on trial and convicted will be my therapy. Nikki is worried that seeing him will completely break me. Neither of their thoughts mirrors what's on my mind.

I close my eyes. The moonlight breaks through the darkness, and then I see it again. The gun. His finger. His face. I look into his eyes, into the eyes of my shooter, into the eyes of who isn't Bruce.

CHAPTER 4

Nikki's grip is secure, almost uncomfortable, but I don't pull away. She wants me to feel supported and I appreciate that. I need that.

"Nervous?"

I shake my head as we step into the hall. We spent hours in the closet, and I didn't have my phone at my side. I missed my mother's texts, her calls. I had planned to walk Nikki out before my mother arrived, but time got away from me, from us, and my mother is here. Aunt Linda has returned.

As Nikki and I head for the living room, hand in hand, I brace myself for my mother's words. Though both she and Aunt Linda have become more open about me spending one-on-one time with Nikki, my mother isn't likely to be too kind about me not responding to her texts, about me not meeting and greeting her at the door. She's not likely to be too understanding about finding Nikki and I huddled up on the closet floor, completely unprepared for her visit.

Nikki and I step into the living room. My mother and my aunt sit side by side.

I speak first. "Sorry. I lost track of time."

"I reckon you lost track of your phone as well," Aunt Linda says, the sweetness not present in her voice. "I told you that your mother would be stopping by."

"It wasn't beside me. I didn't hear it. I'm sorry."

"He fell asleep," Nikki says. "He's overwhelmed, and he needed to escape for a minute."

"That's what prayer is for," Aunt Linda says. "You need relief, an answer, an ear? You talk to God. You don't hide in closets with your friends. You don't keep your elders waiting."

Nikki releases an exhausted sigh. She's bitten her tongue for years. We both have. But she's been much more outspoken lately, after all that's happened to me. Our belief in God is still strong, but our frustrations with our families, our clergy, and our neighbors have grown so high we've lost our ability to remain silent, meek, and accepting of all they require of us. I pray, and so does Nikki. But still, we feel. We face internal struggles. We deal with confusions. We need to be able to deal with them like normal human beings. Prayer can be a part of that, but we should be allowed to cry, hide, take breaks, express anger, be different, be ourselves and feel our feelings without criticism.

Again, Nikki sighs loudly. Her hand is still holding tightly onto mine. "He's been through so much. More than any of us could ever understand because we're on the outside. He has to actually feel it, face all the scary images inside his head, and live with a fear we're lucky we don't have. Why is it so hard to lighten up on him? I get it, okay? I get it." She nods. "God will listen. God will provide. I get that, even believe that, but I also believe my friend…" Nikki stops speaking, looks away from my aunt and into my eyes. "I believe my friend deserves a lot better than he's getting from his family and church. More than scripture readings, pills, and a room he wasn't shot in, he deserves hugs, understanding, and the freedom to hide wherever and whenever he feels the need to." Nikki looks at my mother. "He was shot. A bullet went into his chest while he was in the place he should've felt safest. His home."

My insides heat up. My heart punches against my chest. Tears well in my eyes. I close them quickly. The gun appears. I re-open them in a hurry, before the shot fires.

I squeeze Nikki's hand, use my other hand to massage my churning stomach.

Sweat begins to escape my chest. I can feel drops slowly running down my body beneath my shirt.

I'm hot. So hot. I feel sick. I'm exhausted, but sleep is the most unpleasant place for me. I want to cry, but can't right now. Not in front of them. I don't want them to begin reciting scriptures I already have memorized or to call Dr. Benson.

"You okay?" Nikki asks, moving in closer to my face, never releasing my hand.

I nod, with my eyes on hers. "I'm fine."

I look to my mother. Her eyes are on me, but she hasn't spoken. She probably doesn't know what to say. She surely doesn't know how to comfort me. I'm her son, but not the one she thought I was. This son, the one who is gay and had sex with a man he met online, is a stranger to her.

"You ought to head home, Nikolette," Aunt Linda says. "We appreciate your support, but I think Joseph could use some alone time with his mother."

"Stay with me," Nikki tells me, ignoring my

aunt. "You're not alone. I'm here. Breathe. Deep breaths," she encourages.

I take slow deep breaths, my eyes on my friend's.

Aunt Linda stands. "Nikolette."

"I'll walk her out," I say.

My sweaty hand is glued to hers as we move toward the front door. With each step, my already bleeding heart takes another stab. I don't want to say goodbye to Nikki. I don't want to watch her turn around, give me her back, even though not by choice, and walk away. I want Nikki to stay. I always want her near. I can do without anyone else, but Nikki is my heart, and like anyone else, we all need our hearts to stay healthy, to feel love, to stay alive.

At the door, I pull my hand from her grasp and wrap her in a tight embrace. I pull her head to my chest, silently hope she realizes that the beat she's listening to can only be heard because her consistent, sincere love has kept my broken heart pumping. I inhale her scent, the faint smell of baby lotion, the only moisturizer she's unafraid to use on her extra-sensitive skin. I whisper, "I love you."

"Love you too, JJ. Please call me if you need to and please look at tomorrow for what it is. It's the beginning of the end. This trial is going to play out, and yes it will be difficult, but it all leads up to a verdict that'll be the needed period at the end of this horrible chapter. This trial will be over before you know it, will make the media uninterested in you because there will be nothing else to talk about, will convict your attempted murderer, and will set you free of this. Then, you can move on, and I can help you through the emotional stuff. The period puts an end to all of this but leads right to our start as new, but free adults," she says in a low voice. "I love you," she says again. "Your family, your real family, is right here."

I kiss her cheek before letting my arms fall from around her. I look at her beautiful, brown, angelic face. I look at who has the biggest heart on this planet, whose loyalty is unwavering, whose kindness knows no bounds. I look at who I watched get baptized, the one who obeys her parents, who takes her education and life seriously, who wants to do her part to make this world a better place, yet this town is trying to hold hostage. I applaud Nikki for silently making plans, for choosing her own path, for always standing up for what's right, and never letting the frustrations of growing up in such a sheltered, old-fashioned town rob her of her hopefulness and open-heartedness. Her strength is an inspiration. Unfortunately, I've just become too weakened from the constant insults and abundant hatred to model my best friend's behavior. I needed something else. Someone else. *Bruce*. And I got a lot more and a lot less than I set out for.

I open the door and Nikki steps out. A gentle breeze teases her wild, untied hair. The sun kisses her milk chocolate skin, giving her arms a glow. She turns slowly, covers her cross with her left hand, and blows me a kiss with her right. A tear falls from each eye as my stomach cramps, and I blow a kiss back her way. Before she can rush back to wipe my tears, I close the door. I rest my forehead against the thick wood, take a deep breath that forces the shakes out of me, and twist the lock.

"Joseph!" Aunt Linda shouts.

I wipe my tears before dragging my feet back to the living room. My mother hasn't moved, hasn't spoken. Aunt Linda has. She's on her feet, fuming inside I'm sure. The Bible I was pretending to read before she left for church service is now in her hands, only inches from her face.

My mother looks at me, throws her eyes at her sister, and then eyes me again.

"I apologize for keeping you waiting,

Mama."

She nods once, doesn't offer me a lecture, doesn't scold me for being tardy or unready for her visit. She doesn't speak a word.

"How have you been?"

She folds her hands. "Just trying to hold it together."

This time I nod. I don't think shutting me out should've been her decision. She may have chosen her husband and promised to stand beside him through anything, but I'm her son. I wouldn't exist without her. She abandoned me to stand beside my father. That reality burns, and while I'll never be a wife or mother, I don't think that's something I could ever do to my child. Still, I'm not unaware of the fact that my mother has been forced into an awful position. I know this has weighed heavy on her heart. I know this has changed her life in the worst ways. Though I didn't ask to be gay, I know I've disappointed her.

"And you?" she asks. "How are you? Are your medications working?"

I nod, lie to her just as I did my aunt. "The medications are working fine. I took them this morning."

"And you?" she repeats. "How are you feeling, Joseph?"

I decide to tell the truth, to be real and transparent for my mother as my aunt steps out of the room. "Not so good today. I've been feeling..." I stop, don't try to describe what I'm feeling. No word could sum up exactly what's encumbering me, what's making this day the hardest of my life. Recovering from the near-fatal gunshot wound was easier. My survival was left up to professionals. Getting through this day, this conversation, and staying calm while unsought images appear in my head depends on me.

"It's the trial," she says. "You're anxious about tomorrow. I expected you to be feeling some kind of way. That's why I stopped by to check in. Did y'all discuss it? You and Nikolette?"

I nod. "A little. She offered me encouragement."

"Will she be present?"

"No. I thought it best that she offer her support from a distance."

My mother nods. "I agree. We don't need this to turn into even more of a circus. It used to be a blessing that our town was so small, and I loved knowing that whenever I decided to read about what was going on in the world, no matter what, I knew the news wouldn't be covering anyone I knew." Her head falls in shame. She brings her folded hands up to her face, appears as though she's praying. "Now, this town doesn't feel small. It doesn't feel comfortable. I feel boxed in. Trapped. Everyone's talking about..." She stops speaking. She exhales but doesn't look or sound relieved. "Everyone's putting their spin on my family's tragedy, creating their own opinions about what I did wrong with my son. They're all..."

I interrupt her. "You never did anything wrong. I don't care what they're saying or what they believe. You didn't make me this way." I look at my mother, but her eyes are on her hands. I continue speaking, though I don't know if she's praying or listening to me. "I know you don't understand it, but I've always been this way. You can't just wake up gay."

"Stop it! We're not going there, Joseph." She stands, holds her hand out in front of my face. "I can't take it. I can't hear this right now. I just can't." Her voice cracks terribly. Her butterscotch complexion flushes as tears escape her eyes.

I stand too, tower over my mother's small frame. I want to wipe her tears, to touch her reddened face, but I don't reach out. I don't know if she'd push me away. I don't know if she'd reject me, and that's something I can't take again. I want to comfort her, to at least try. I want to show my mother that even in her absence, I still love her. I forgive her. I want to make her believe that carrying fault isn't something she should have to do. It certainly isn't what she deserves no matter how her actions have made me feel.

I grab my chest. Heartache falls from my eyes as well. "I want to hug you, Mama, but I don't know if I'm allowed to, if you want me to." With the back of my hand, I rub the tears from my face. "I hate to see you sad." I sniff hard before anything can fall from my nose. "I love you, Mama, and I'm sorry I've disappointed you."

She looks me in the eye. She doesn't accept or reject my apology. She doesn't comment at all, not even to tell me a hug isn't necessary. I don't know what to do. I'm stuck in place with my eye on my mother, a knot in my gut, and a gallon of uncertainty burdening my heart.

My mother puts her hand out again. "I want to talk to you, to find out about how you've been, but I can't do the gay stuff right now, Joseph. I just can't."

The gay stuff. I resist shaking my head and showing disrespect. *Stuff.* Such a disrespectful way to describe my sexual orientation, what has made me a pariah in my own town, what almost got me killed. I think of stuff as what's left lying on a kid's floor, the nonsense that clutters the bottom of a woman's bag. I don't think of my sexual orientation, what determines the gender I'm attracted to, as *stuff*.

I sit back down, and only seconds later, she does the same.

"I'd like to see you return to church."

"I'm not welcome," I respond immediately.

"Did God tell you that?"

No, but everyone else has. "No one wants me there. Sitting there and hearing the whispers, seeing the dirty looks, and feeling the judgment is too much, especially after what happened."

"The entire church prayed for your recovery, Joseph."

"No, I'm sure they simply bowed their heads."

"Do you want to hurt me? Do you want me to leave?"

I look at my mother's face. Like my Aunt Linda, she's a special kind of ignorant. She too thinks exactly like her pastor, her husband. I shake my head, my eyes still on her. "No, Mama. Never have I wanted to hurt you."

"You want me to think like you, to welcome

sin, to accept this new way of living you youngsters are trying to normalize?"

"New? There's nothing even slightly new about homosexuality. It's not some new concept a couple of kids thought up some years back, and it caught on. It's real. I know it is. It's in me. I've been attracted to boys since before I even realized what I was experiencing were crushes."

She stands again, her hand back out, shushing me and keeping me at arm's length. "I wanted to be here to support you before your trial. I wanted to check in. I wanted to pray with you. But you want to go down a path I'm not willing to go down with you. I love you, Joseph. Deeply. But this isn't the topic for me. You want to pray about it? I'm all in. You want to share your stories, your understandings, your opinions? I'm not willing to listen or respond to what goes against my beliefs."

I don't say a thing. I can't apologize any more than I already have. I can't create any new prayers, begging to wake up straight. Clearly, this is who I'm meant to be, and because of that, I can't keep saying sorry. I'm gay, was born this way. It's not something I'm comfortable shouting from the mountaintops, but it's something I must own. It's something I must repeat to myself. I wouldn't hurt anyone, wouldn't even hurt an animal, so I can't keep allowing these people, my people, to make me feel like I'm a pervert, a demon. I'm gay, but not inhuman. My heart wants to love, and like anyone, I want to feel loved. I just want to receive my love from a man.

"Can we pray, Joseph?"

I look at my mother and my stomach twists in a sickening way. Tears fall that I didn't even feel build. I clutch my stomach, let my head fall, close my eyes, beg my mind to produce an image of Nikki, my everything. For once, I see what I want. Not the gun. I see Nikki's beautiful face, her calming, reassuring smile. Then, like a solar eclipse, my sun is blocked. The darkness is brief and then I see the revolver. I force myself to open my eyes, to return to my reality before the trigger is pulled. My mother is still standing, waiting for an answer.

I want to speak, but no answer will bring me satisfaction. Her prayer will beg for the lord to change me, will be filled with her apologies, will hurt me throughout, will go on for minutes that'll feel like hours. Saying yes will result in me hearing that I'm not the kind of son she wished for me to be, that she's sorry for whatever she did to birth someone like me, and that me becoming heterosexual and Bruce receiving a guilty verdict are our only hopes for a normal life. I can't sit through that.

Saying no isn't any better. She'll leave with more pain in her heart than she came with, and I'll mentally beat myself up about my answer for the rest of the day. No matter how differently we view this situation, this woman raised me. She's my mother. I love her.

"Maybe it's best that your father has decided to come see you this evening."

My eyes bulge. My heart briefly stops. I grab at my chest, hit myself once, force the beat to come back. It does. Erratically.

"He's blessed, Joseph. He has a way of delivering the word so that it really touches people. I think hearing him after all this time will be helpful, will make waking up tomorrow morning and facing the trial easier."

I shake my head frantically. I envision my closet, where I so badly want to be right now. I consider what could happen if my mother leaves me alone with him. I jump up from my seat, grab her with an unsteady hand. My head still shaking, I say, "No."

"No what? Joseph, sit down."

"No," I say again, my vision going in and out. "I need you here, for you to pray with me. Not him. You." I nod, can feel the sweat pouring out of me from all over. "Yes, Mama. You can pray with me."

She gently pushes me back down to my seat. Barely able to see, barely able to breathe, I bow my head. She speaks words that begin to fade along with my ability to focus. Loudly, I hear the gunshot, the echo, the ringing in my ears. *Nikki. Please, Nikki. Come back.*

I close my eyes tightly before reopening them. With clearer vision and my head still bowed, I see my mother's hands holding mine. I can't feel her touch, but I can see her hands. It's Nikki's hands I wish I were looking at, but I'm grateful that my mother is with me. She's here, and I'll beg for prayer for the rest of the day if I must. I'll say whatever is necessary to keep my mother in this room, to keep from being left alone for even a second with my father. My shooter.

CHAPTER 5

My shirt is drenched. My head is throbbing. My neck is sore, but I refuse to lift my head. My mother thought a few prayers would be enough, but I made it clear that they weren't, and as I requested, she's now reading the word to me. I won't let her leave, refuse to take any chances. I should've known he'd want to see me today, the day before the trial begins. Bruce's only wrongdoings were taking advantage of my emotions and using my body for his own selfish pleasures. He's guilty of heartbreak. He's not guilty of what he's being accused of. The town's pastor, the man who still lies beside my mother at night, the man who is the reason I exist, aimed for my heart, and tried to end what he helped to create. My life.

My mother's voice sounds so distant as my mind takes me back to an evening I now realize is when I made the greatest mistake of my life.

Not the evening I spent with Bruce, but the evening I ended all suspicion. The evening I looked my father in the eye and admitted I'm homosexual. The evening I threw my relationship with Bruce in my father's face, unaware at the time that the love was one-sided.

My heart had become so heavy. Messages were no longer waiting on my phone for me from Bruce. The insults and cutting stares had begun to hurt more than ever before. Bruce felt so far from me, but my hopes were still high, and my heart was still his. During that time, my father was becoming frustrated with the changes he was seeing in me. For months, Bruce and I spoke daily, and his words, his love, and his attention gave me the strength to smile through my miserable daily reality. Without hearing Bruce's voice and reading his words, all I could do was wait impatiently to hear from him and question what had happened to what we built. But I couldn't find the strength to smile anymore, to appear eager to participate in church functions anymore, to even eat a full meal with my parents. Heartbreak is the worst of all pains, and though I was trying to believe in Bruce, I couldn't fake happiness in my home any longer.

My father had grown tired of seeing me so

depressed. The rumors that were circulating were constantly jabbing at him. He was dealing with his own daily torture. He felt as though the whispers didn't only question me, but him too as a pastor, as a man, and as a father. Here in this town, homosexuality is thought to be a choice. He just knew that everyone blamed him for my *sick* decision making.

A dinner I had tried to excuse myself from became somewhat of a Last Supper for me. My father, at the head of the table, attacked me with his wicked stare the moment I sat down. Instead of looking away, I maintained strong eye contact, watched him emotionlessly. I never picked up my fork to take one bite of the meatloaf. I never took one sip of my water. My eyes were on my father's, awaiting his words.

He never spoke, and though eye contact was still held, I grew tired of staring at him, waiting, feeling threatened by my own parent. I wanted to get up, go to my room, be surprised by a text message I had prayed would be waiting for me.

I asked, "Can I please be excused?"

My mother didn't answer. My father didn't either.

"Please," I added, my eyes still on my father's.

"Why? So you can go upstairs, hide in your room, pretend to be studying when you're involved in some sort of faggotry?"

Faggotry. The most ignorant and insulting word my father casually throws around in reference to homosexual behavior of any sort.

I didn't comment, didn't defend myself, nor question what he could've known.

"I've wised up to something," he said.

I felt my entire body shudder. I had hoped he didn't notice. The last thing I wanted him to sense, to pick up on, was my fear. But I could feel it, the fear, traveling through my veins, intensifying, forcing my legs and arms to repetitively twitch.

Hands clasped, elbows resting on the table, he leaned forward, over his plate, and narrowed his eyes as he spoke. "I've been asking myself why, of all the other young men, would they pick my boy to spread lies about. So, I started watching you. You're not soft because of your mama." He shook his head. "You're not an outcast because you're my son. No." He shook his head again. "You were targeted because they could see what I couldn't. They saw what I was blind to because I never considered, for even a second, that I could raise a queer. A damn faggot."

My heart had begun to slam against my chest. I remember realizing that the fear had dissipated, only to quickly be replaced with anger. *Queer. Faggot.* So many labels when all I wanted, and still want, is to be called by my name.

"You brought the devil into my house, boy!" he yelled, making my mother jump. "You brought the devil into my church!" He stood, and I hurried to my feet to avoid having to look up to him, something I hated having to always do.

"Please," my mother cried out.

My father's eyes stayed on mine. "I see it! There's truth in it, in everything they say."

I straightened my back and kept my eyes on his, hoping to appear strong, though his standing had put terror back in me.

"Be a man, Joseph. Say it!"

He stepped around the table and positioned himself in front of me. I could feel his breath on my face, could feel the heat radiating from his body. He stood in front of me. Eyes that I inherited pierced mine.

"You a coward too?" he asked. "A faggot and a coward?"

Every word, a slice into my soul. My father was standing before me, in my face, bigger bodied than me, an aggressor, attacking me for something I couldn't control and couldn't hide well. I could feel my body quivering, could feel it all building in my eyes, but crying would've made it a million times worse. It'd have given him an answer. A *yes*. My tears would've made me look like the coward he was asking me to call myself, but breaking down would've infuriated him more.

In a swift motion, with a firm open palm, he whipped his hand across my cheek.

The sting made me want to cry, to strike him back, to curse him for pretending he was this great man, but finding it okay to treat me in such a way.

"I asked you a question!" he said. Spit sprayed into my face as he yelled. "You a coward, too? Or just a faggot? Say it. Be man enough to say what you are." With the back of his hand, he struck the other side of my face.

"Yes!" I answered as loudly as I could. Face to face, inches from my father, my height mirroring his, I gave him the truth. "I'm gay. I'm what they say, have been forever, and yes, I came from you."

He balled up his fist, prepared to knock me out cold, I'm sure, but my mother jumped up. She grabbed his arm, tried to convince him that I was talking crazy, that my words were untrue.

"It's the truth. I'm gay! I may not have anyone in this damn town, but I have a boyfriend. Someone out there loves me and he's waiting for me," I revealed. Both sides of my face stung, and lord knows I didn't want to take another hit, but remaining silent wasn't something I could do any longer. "And I love him too. He wants me to move in with him. He wants a life with me. He wants to finish what we've started, and I can't wait to."

My mother released his fist, and it fell to his side. Her head fell, and so did her tears. My father never looked away. He grimaced in a disturbing way. The surprise and disgust turned his lips downward, forced his eyes to squint until they were nearly closed, made his large chest rise and fall. He was seething. He was shocked. He was revolted by my words.

My father took a step back, placed his arm around my mother, but kept his eyes on me. Eyes, that I got from him, suddenly looked black, emotionless, unrecognizable. I wasn't in them. My father's eyes were on me, but he wasn't looking at his son. He wasn't seeing a person. I realized right away that I had made a mistake. My father was begging for truth, but deep down, he needed to hear me deny the rumors. He needed me to tell more lies. I didn't. I shared everything. Facts and what I was still hopeful for. I didn't know if Bruce was still waiting for me. I couldn't read nor understand his silence, but I had to hold onto something, and at that moment, more than ever, I needed him.

I left the kitchen, locked myself in my room, and grabbed my phone before sitting on the side of my bed. My display showed that one message was waiting for me. My heart fluttered. My fingers couldn't unlock my phone fast enough. I couldn't wait to read what he had sent me. Only, he hadn't sent me anything. It was from Nikki. Bruce was still maintaining his cruel silence.

Tears fell, loud crying came out of me as I texted him. *Why won't you talk to me? You have no idea how much I love you and need you. I told my father about us. Whatever I did to upset you, or whatever you're going through, we have to deal with later. I need you now. I can't stay here. I've stopped hiding. You said, one day I'm going to say fuck it and tell the world. I didn't tell the world, but I manned up and told my father. You told me before that you wanted to be a part of my journey and wanted to be the one to hold my hand while I come out the closet. Hold my hand, Bruce. Please.*

I stopped typing, sent the message, and

waited for Bruce's response. My body was shaking all over. My heart was beating at an unhealthily fast rate.

I heard my parent's bedroom door slam and I could hear my mother emotionally breaking down because of me, because of what I revealed to them. I stared at my phone. My tears fell on the screen, but I never pulled my eyes away, never wiped the fallen drops. I waited for his reply, waited for him to tell me that he had been waiting to hear that, to tell me he was coming to rescue me. He didn't say any of that. His reply was vicious. It broke me into smaller pieces. Pieces I still haven't been able to glue back together.

Bruce replied in all caps, like a screaming teenager. He offered me no explanation for the silent treatment. He didn't tell me he was proud of me for telling my father the truth. He didn't ask me anything, not even what details I shared with my father. He sent me callousness, a harsh rejection. His words have been seared into my mind and unfortunately, my heart. He wrote, *TYPICALLY, WHEN PEOPLE DON'T GET RESPONSES, THEY STOP TALKING. YOU DON'T, SO MAYBE I SHOULD BE MORE DIRECT. LEAVE ME ALONE, JOSEPH! THINGS DIDN'T WORK OUT AND THEY'RE NOT GO-*

ING TO. DON'T TELL YOUR FATHER ANY-THING ELSE. LEAVE MY NAME OUT OF WHATEVER YOU SAY. DON'T MAKE YOUR LIFE OR MINE MORE DIFFICULT. STOP TEX-TING ME!

I remember wailing loudly, pressing against my chest, trying to stop what felt like my heart falling out. I remember hearing myself cry out in sporadic bursts. It wouldn't all come out at once. I couldn't release all the pain in one full cry. I was breaking in every way. Slowly.

Heartbreak isn't fast, isn't brief, isn't un-complicated. It's an experience. It's sickening, traumatic, dreadful. You break bit by bit until you feel irreparable. You feel like you're dying, but death, the end result, the finale, never ar-rives.

I pulled my hand from my chest, and reread Bruce's hurtful reply. I couldn't stop texting him. He gave me light and then put me back in the dark. And for what? For one night? To be my first? There were guys online selling their first experiences. Why take mine in this way? I typed, *I'm going to tell everyone. I'll take another hit, but I'm going to tell my father. I'm going to post all over Craigslist what kind of "man" you are. You took advantage of my heart, used my vulnerability, my body, and now you're trying to walk out of my life like nothing ever happened. You're acting as if you never told me you loved me. You're acting like I meant nothing. I won't let you do this to anyone else.*

After sending my words his way, I dropped the phone, fell back on the bed, and covered my face with both hands. I breathed into my palms, cried behind my hands, and choked on my own sorrows. At that moment, I wished Bruce had never answered my ad. Up until then, unbelievably, I was able to hold onto hope. He robbed me of all hopefulness with his nasty reply. He introduced me to a different type of loneliness, one blacker and more haunting than the one my neighbors and classmates introduced me to.

I cried, lying on my bed alone, on a bed where Bruce and I had an experience I thought solidified something. I cried until my phone beeped, pulling my attention its way. It was a message from Bruce. It was the last message I've ever received from him, a message that I've been questioned about, a message that'll be used in court. Still using all caps, he wrote, *YOU MUST WANT ME TO SHUT YOUR MOUTH FOR YOU.*

I didn't reply to him, didn't reach out to Nikki for support, didn't check on my mother, didn't visit the bathroom to look at my face in the mirror, though I could feel raised welts on my cheeks. I didn't shower, brush my teeth, or prepare for the night at all. I didn't leave my room again until later that night when I was being wheeled out on a stretcher.

I never got the chance to close my eyes and recover from the day. I never got to apologize to my mother for breaking her heart. I never got to make good on my threats to tell the world about Bruce. I never even got to think about what my father would do to me or say to me the next time we'd be forced to stand face to face. I found out, though. Later that night, no time to ponder about it, at the hands of my father, I got a life-changing, near life-ending surprise. A shot to the chest.

CHAPTER 6

Still drenched in my own sweat, I sit with my head lowered. My mother reads in a slow, calming voice. A voice that's pulled me out of my mind, away from my memories of *that* night, and brought me back into this room. I listen to words my father has recited countless times, words that he claims to follow. I listen to scriptures that have been committed to memory, to words that I believe, that I turn to for comfort and strength. I sit silently, taking in earfuls of what my mother feels I need to hear right now, mostly scriptures from Psalms and Philippians.

I hold onto my mother's voice. I keep my eyes on the floor and make my blinks as brief as possible. I don't want to see anything else. I don't want to end up on another carousel ride inside my brain. I want to get through this. I want to face my father with my mother present, get this over with, and return to my closet.

"Joseph."

I make eye contact with my mother. Held out in front of her is a small pouch of Kleenex.

"You're sweating profusely," she says.

I take the tissues from her hand, use a couple to wipe my face clean, and hand her the pouch back. "Thank you, Mama."

She closes her bible, and I prepare to beg, cry, grab her leg if I must to keep her in this room.

"How are you feeling? Any better?"

I nod, though I'm tempted to say no. I don't feel better, but I don't want her to feel unappreciated, as though her efforts did nothing for me.

"Good." She reaches forward and peels a small piece of sweat-soaked tissue from my forehead. "The power of prayer, huh?"

Two strong knocks make me jump before I can respond to her. My mother quickly rises to her feet and moves toward the door.

It's him. My father. My monster. He hasn't entered this room yet, hasn't even walked inside the house, but his presence being this close is so heavy, so unsettling for me, it nearly takes my vision, my heartbeat, my ability to feel the body I'm in. Everything is numb. My legs, my arms, my fingers. My sight goes in and out, like a light being turned off and on. I can hear my breath sputtering in and out of me like a struggling old engine trying to turn over.

Nikki. Please, Nikki. I need to hear you. I need to see your face. I lose my vision again, see nothing but complete blackness, don't get even a glimpse of my much-needed friend's face. I fear that I've passed out, but I can still hear my breathing, can still hear my thoughts, my pleads to see something, someone, truly beautiful. My Nikki.

No sight, not even blurred visuals. I can't see a thing but can feel myself blinking. My surroundings become blazing hot, like I'm being cremated while still alive. My breathing stops. Or my hearing does. I'm not sure which, but my difficult breaths can no longer be heard.

What's happening? Open your eyes, Joseph. Don't slip away. That I could hear. I can hear my thoughts, my silent questions, my own confusion. Perhaps, this is hell. The devil did just arrive.

* * *

Still so hot. My entire body is a furnace, but I can feel my face again. I can feel cold breaking through, touching my skin, bringing me back enough to hear my breathing again. Cold drops run down my face, glide down my neck, make my face twitch.

"Can you hear me?" she asks. Her voice sounds near, right by my ear.

I know my mother's voice, and that's not it. That's Aunt Linda.

"Joseph, can you hear me?"

I force my head to move, hope that it looks to her like a nod.

"Open your eyes."

I can hear my aunt, want to do as she's asked, but even opening my eyes seems like an impossible task. My energy, every bit of it, left me the moment he darkened the doorstep. Opening my eyes to do something as simple as look at where I am and who's surrounding me seems too overwhelming to achieve.

"Try," she says.

I breathe in a chest full of air before releasing it slowly. Again, I do that before making the taxing attempt to separate eyelids that feel glued together.

Open your eyes, Joseph. Focus.

"Come on, Joseph," Aunt Linda says, separating my left lids with her thumb and forefinger. "I need to make sure you've come to."

Come to? I passed out. For how long, I don't know. But I was left most vulnerable around the man who nearly killed me. I was in a defenseless position that could've earned me a brutal beating had my mother and aunt not been here.

With my lids being held apart, my eye drifts to the left and pulls in a hazy, but distinguishable image of my aunt.

"Can you see me?"

"Yes," I say, almost inaudibly.

She allows my eye to close. Without her assistance, without using my own fingers, I force myself to open both eyes.

Everything is fuzzy. Though sitting, I don't feel stable, like I'm sitting still.

Cool breezes hit my face. I blink a few times. Slow, long blinks until I'm able to see my mother. Her small frame is positioned in front of me. With a church program, she fans me, creating cool gusts that help to bring back feeling and clearer vision.

"Drink," my aunt demands.

I part my lips and in pours cool water. My body welcomes it. In large swallows, I gulp more until there's no more to drink.

I slowly bring my hands to my face and rub my eyes. I take a deep breath, listen to myself release hot air as cool winds continue to brush across me.

I reopen my eyes and see my mother, my vision no longer cloudy. I look at my aunt. Her eyes are wide and on me. In one hand is the empty glass and in the other is a washcloth, water dripping from it onto the floor.

"Thank you," I say in a low voice.

"I thought you were going to need to go to the hospital. I didn't know what was happening. Your eyes were open. You were talking," my aunt explains. "You were calling out for Nikki. Then you went silent. Sweat was pouring out of you. You weren't responding to us. You blacked out."

"For how long?" I ask.

My mother stops fanning me and places the church program on the table. "Not long. A few minutes. Enough time to make me consider sending you to the hospital."

"I didn't mean to scare you."

"You've got to learn to communicate what you feel so you don't lose yourself, so you don't have incidences like this. Isn't that what Dr. Benson has been speaking to you about? I thought your medications were helping. You shouldn't be having blackouts."

My aunt's voice is tender, but her words sound scolding. I can't communicate what I'm feeling because there are no words, none that could ever fully convey what's going on inside me. I can't talk it out because the truth, my truth, will either be too hard to believe or will be too crushing to my mother for me to say aloud and publicly share. I can't take the pills, can't speak about the hole in my chest, can't talk about the pain in my heart, or the horror movie my mind replays every day because everyone's method of comfort will be to verbally attack a man I once loved because of what my father, a man they love and adore, did to me. I need solace, but they don't know how to give it to someone like me. They can't empathize with me, and they can't sympathize with a homosexual because they fear that'd make them questionable Christians. Hateful slurs as hard-hitting as the bullet that nearly killed me is all they can shoot my way. Though they're all aimed at Bruce, they hit me too, destroy me piece by piece, because no matter what they believe he did to me, his greatest crime in their eyes is being a gay man. And I'm gay, too.

"You should call Dr. Benson. He said he'd be available to you by phone. He knew these last few days before the trial would weigh heavy on you and trigger more emotion than you normally experience."

I shake my head, reject my aunt's suggestion immediately. "I'm okay. I don't need to call him."

"Are you ready to speak with your father?" my mother asks.

My father. The man who shot me and turned around so casually as if he just tossed a piece a garbage in the trash bin on his way out. The man who knew I was in this room falling apart and didn't even step in to pretend he cares. The man who sleeps with his hand resting on a holy book, but preaches hate and encourages judgment. The man who is willing to remain silent while another man rots away in prison for a crime he didn't commit. *My father.* The man I wish to be nothing like.

I don't answer my mother, and she doesn't stand patiently awaiting a response. She walks toward the kitchen, leaving me alone with my aunt.

"This will be good for you, Joseph," my aunt says surely before stepping out of the room with the empty glass and dripping cloth in hand.

Alone, I sit and begin to feel myself coming back to life inside my body. I can feel my limbs and the intense uneasiness of my nerves. I can feel dread covering me as I hear them, him, heading my way.

Like the grim reaper and the feeling surrounding him as an entity, my father encompasses all things dark. His shadow is jolting. His presence is unwelcome, terrifying, and like the supposed skeleton floating around beneath a black cloak, my father is the robber of life.

In he walks, alongside my mother, dressed in an all-black suit, holding a black bible with several colorful flags sticking out from all sides. He sits across from me, where my mother sat to read selected scriptures. His eyes stare intently into mine. His nostrils flare, jaw tenses, face twitches in what I can only consider complete hatred. There's no remorse to be read on his face, but I can see that he loathes me even more now than he did before.

I shift in my seat, take a deep breath, open and close my fists, make sure I can still feel my body, that I don't fall out again, not when he's this close. I'm sitting only feet away from my shooter. My shooter is sitting before his son, the person he failed to end, had hoped to never see again.

I'm irreversibly damaged, full of sadness, and empty of all aspirations because of how I've been treated by those who've raised me, because of how those who've grown up with me act toward me, because of how I've been criticized, and how I'm still spoken to and about. From the outside looking in, we don't look like an unprogressive, ignorant town. We look wholesome, loving, and it's thought to be a positive attribute of our community that we haven't changed with the times. No twerking videos, recorded fights, or sex tapes would ever be filmed in this town or feature any of our residents. And it's simply incomprehensible that our pastor would cause anyone any harm, especially his own child. This town wears the single best disguise that exists. It's masked behind what was never supposed to become an excuse, but what we're supposed to be grounded in, regardless of who or what we believe in. Religion.

I wait for him to speak, though I can't imagine what he could say. No way am I going to open my mouth first. I'd rather not have to see or speak to him at all, but if I must, I'm not taking on the chore of *breaking the ice.*

My father clears his throat. "God has never left your side. That's why you're still here."

I don't move or say a word. I've thanked God countless times. I did so from my hospital bed, while eating, while lying in my closet. I don't need to respond to my father's statement. I don't need to thank God in front of him just so he can convince himself that it was because of him that I chose to do so. I know God has never left me. I also know who did.

"Tomorrow, you shouldn't leave his side."

I can feel my eyes narrow as confusion takes over.

With my mother's hand resting on my father's shoulder, he says, "God has never left you, so don't walk away from Him. Standing by the wrong person tomorrow is the perfect way to show your ungratefulness for all He's done for you."

The wrong person. In my father's eyes, the man I was sexually involved with will always be at greater fault, though he was the one who fired the shot. My father will always believe that his sin is more forgivable, that his attempt on my life isn't as bad because he's a man who doesn't sleep with other men.

"Are you planning to do what's right, to push your feelings to the side, and tell the truth about the man who put you in the position you're in?"

I maintain eye contact with my father. He grips his bible, awaiting an answer I don't plan to give.

"Had he not started a relationship with a teenager, lived his life as a sick pervert, you wouldn't be where you are right now. You wouldn't have ended up shot. You wouldn't be going to court tomorrow. You wouldn't have to face a jury, relive what happened to you, disappoint your mama with the choices you've made."

My father, the man behind the .22 millimeter, the finger on the trigger, the committer of the crime, put a bullet in my chest, now he's stabbing me directly in the heart. He inserted the blade by putting all the blame on Bruce, then twisted it by pointing out the disappointment I've caused my mother, and will continue to cause her as she sits through the trial. She may have given all her attention to my father throughout the last several months. She may have given him the support I was in dire need of, comforted and showered the wrong person with affection, but I've never stopped loving her, not even while I felt completely parentless. Through all the anger, feelings of abandonment, and even shame for what I can't control, I've never stopped loving my mama. Not even for a second.

"Your mama needs peace," he says twisting the blade again, hitting me deeper than the bullet ever went.

My eyes move to my mother. Her teary eyes do more damage than Bruce ever did, than my father ever did, than this town ever did. She raised me to remain strong in my faith, pray every day, and be myself. That's all I've been trying to be, but the me I am doesn't add up to the son she wants. I'm obedient, God-fearing, and God-serving. I'm an academic achiever. I'm respectful to all. But I'm gay. Being homosexual erases everything else about me, no matter how good. That's a concept I can't fathom, but a reality I must constantly swallow.

"Are you hearing me?" he asks, pulling my eyes back to him. "Your mama needs for the trial to end as soon as possible, for the media to stop focusing on this family. She needs me," he says, lowering his volume significantly.

A few tears fall. *She needs me.* I know exactly what that means, why he's here, what he's asking of me. He's asking me, while clutching a bible, to allow an innocent man to spend years in prison for what he didn't do. He's asking me to save his life, his reputation, his marriage to my mother, by letting Bruce take the fall for something he never did.

"She needs me to get back to who I used to be." His regular speaking voice returns.

I glance at my mother. Her tears have fallen. Maybe they fell when mine did. I look back at my father, at someone I'd be okay never sitting across from again, okay never seeing again. The last time I looked this man in the eye, he had a gun in his hand. Today, almost a year later, he's asking me to let the unthinkable happen. I don't think it's right that he still gets to remain a hero in my mother's eyes, only looked at as a father who doesn't know how to reach his confused son. It's completely unfair, yet I've pondered for months, and still can't seem to find the strength to turn him in, to tell the truth, to rip him from my mother who would be completely lost without him, who'd lose herself if she suddenly lost her husband, her first and only love. She'd rather be childless than spouseless, which is why her hand is resting on his shoulder and not mine.

I don't attempt to hold the rest of my tears in. I'm done fighting with myself. I let them all run, slide down my cheeks, unwiped. This hurts. It's a losing battle no matter what. Turning him in will free Bruce, but kill my mother. Ruin her. Letting Bruce be convicted will haunt me for the rest of this life and the next. I wish, as I have so many times before while alone in my closet, that I could just disappear, that I could end all this suffering, end the cruel cycle of thoughts, set both of my parents, even *him*, free of me.

I look at my mother. Not him. I look at her tears, bite my lip as more of my own fall. I've tried so hard to let Nikki's positivity and strength set in and dominate my thoughts, but it seems impossible. The trial is so close. People's lives rest in my hands. My mother's heart does as well. This weight is unbearable.

I take a deep breath, my eyes still on my mother as I force myself to block out the sight of who sickens me, whose presence is petrifying, who's still killing me even though he isn't wielding a gun at this moment.

I push myself up from my seat. Blacking out again is something I'd like to avoid. I stand, shudder as a chill runs through my body. I feel sticky, sweaty, suddenly cold.

I keep my eyes on the woman who carried me. I don't wipe my face, don't force a smile. I focus on standing, pray for the strength to make it back to the closet, to my only sanctuary.

I can't just walk away. That'd be rude to her. I can't go in for a hug. It's not something she'd be receptive to.

I swallow, exhale quietly, look at her worn, flushed face. "I know what I have to do, Mama."

I turn, leave the living room, walk away from my parents, head for my safe zone, my only place to go. As I put one foot in front of the other, moving down the small hallway that seems miles long, Bruce's face flashes before my eyes. I stop briefly and silently ask for forgiveness as I've let him sit in prison awaiting trial for all these months.

I take a quick look behind me, and as expected, notice that no one is there. No one is there to offer me comfort. I'm as alone now as I was the night I was found in my bed and blasted through the chest.

I walk into the room I've been occupying and close myself in. Alone, I stand with my head resting against the wooden door. By myself, I place my hand over my heart. I'm not carrying this because I loved Bruce. I'm not going to court tomorrow because of a breakup that went horribly wrong. I'm standing here, feeling like this, dying inside, struggling to breathe, to stay conscious throughout this day because of the actions of one. *My father*. Because the man whose DNA flows through my veins, who taught me how to catch a ball, who used to love me, would prefer a dead son to a gay one.

CHAPTER 7

Alone. I sit alone in the bottom of the closet, my head tilted back with my eyes on the square door in the ceiling. No one has checked on me, not one of the three of them has asked if I'm okay. I don't want to be with anyone right now, but still, it'd be nice to know that someone cares and is concerned about my current state, especially since I passed out in front of them. I do appreciate quiet, my space, a break from questions, a break from cruel, dishonest persuasion, but knowing that my well-being can be so easily overlooked and disregarded by a whole community of people, my church, and even my parents, makes going into this night less dark and much less frightening than all the other nights I've faced since the evening I was nearly murdered.

I reach to my side and grab the pen and pad I brought into the closet with me. I look at the blankness of the first sheet. No lines. No words.

Just a blank document, awaiting a message, a thought, a sketch, something. Its blankness is a canvas for endless possibilities. At one point, so was my future.

No longer feeling exhausted, lightheaded, overheated, unwell, but assured, I place the point of the pen at the top left of the paper. In the closet, in isolation, my only place to go, I begin. I begin to write a statement I should've made months ago, but didn't. I begin to write what I still won't be able to say tomorrow. *Dear Judge, I've been asked more times than I can count if I was awake when my shooter entered. As many times as I've been asked, I've lied. The truth is, I was awake. I could see who aimed the gun and took the shot. I know who my shooter is, and he is NOT Bruce. I've only been face to face with Bruce one time, months before the night of the shooting, and he's never been a threat to my safety. I've held the truth, which has resulted in Bruce spending months in jail for a crime he didn't commit. I hope God forgives me for what I've allowed to be taken from Bruce. Time, which is something he'll never get back. I hope you do the right thing, use this letter as factual evidence and witness testimony, and set him free. I swear every word is the absolute truth.*

I tear the sheet of paper from the pad after signing my name, fold it in half, and set it on the floor. I take a deep breath, and my feeling of absolute certainty begins to wane as I exhale. I'm finally going to share information that the world should've known months ago, information I thought the police would eventually discover on their own, by checking cell tower data, but Bruce's own words, his angry messages, his lack of an alibi spoke too loudly. I hope my honesty gives him back what he deserves, though my community may not agree. I hope my truthful words give him back his freedom, which he never should've lost, not even for a day, regardless of how badly he broke my heart and ruined my sense of trust. I also hope my truth earns me forgiveness. I've never needed it more.

I look down at the folded paper. Inside are words that'll hopefully save Bruce from an undeserved prison sentence and my mother from living a lonesome life as I didn't implicate the real criminal. Her husband. I look at what will either make me appear honest, strong, and like a do-gooder for stating the facts or like the coward my father has called me more times than I can count because I didn't name who I saw. This letter is asking for the freedom of two men.

I touch the folded sheet, contemplate adding more, then in less than a second, consider ripping it up. I look at the hand I used to write those words, the fingers that printed nothing but what the law requires. The absolute truth. And I do neither, don't rip or write. I stand, say quietly, *so help me God,* push the closet door open, step back into the room, and scan the space slowly.

At the foot of the bed, I look over the quilt, the pillows, the wood paneling, and read the story this room tells. It's an old story, one I can't help but believe will never change and be updated.

I pull the quilt off the bed and fold it before placing it on the closet floor. I grab both flattened pillows that must be used together to give the comfort of one decent pillow and sit them on top of the folded quilt. I look down at the stack I've created, up at the square, and then at the folded note.

With my eyes still on the paper, my hand moves to my throat and I massage it as a sudden sharp pain fills the area, like I swallowed a rock without water, and it got stuck.

I grunt, massage my neck slowly, in downward motions, finding no comfort, the pain not easing up even slightly.

I take a backward step, rest my back against the wall, continue my attempt to rub away a tear-worthy pain that's creating a blurry buildup in my eyes. I blink, feel the tears fall, feel the sharpness remain.

I gasp aloud, fall to my knees, let my face fall into the pillows sitting atop the folded quilt. Into the pillows, I scream out, force the pain to escape, release my cry, yowl, and push the torturous feeling from my throat.

So hot. So hot again. The heat comes over me. I lift my face, pull in fresh, cool air that doesn't feel refreshing, just necessary.

Still so hot. This closet, my only place, the one place that's felt like mine feels like everywhere else in my world. Smothering. Terrifying. Lonely.

I need out. This is a miserable existence, one I can't escape because my anguish goes far beyond my surroundings, but lives in my mind. Plaguing memories constantly replay, with few breaks in between that are awfully short. Medication that's supposed to be helpful sickens me physically. Therapy that encourages open communication is supposed to be relieving, freeing, but how can it be when my doctor carries the same mentality of those who have tormented me endlessly? His door is always open according to him, but he'd rather medicate me than to understand me or actually hear me. Gay guys were not the type of patients he set out to help when he worked toward his license, when he planted his roots in this small town, when he opened his doors to the *public.*

I crawl out of the closet, sweat covering my body again, and inch my way over to my phone. I rest my back on the bed and watch my fingers move insanely fast as I type Nikki's number, as I reach out trying to get ahold of my lifeline. Each time the phone rings, I bawl a little harder. I felt so sure before I began writing that letter, almost relieved about setting free the truth and myself, but ending the letter robbed me of that feeling. The signing of my name, the folding of the paper invited the truth to deliver a harsh slap to my face, to take a firm hold of my neck. Writing out my hidden truth was the equivalent of breaking my love's heart, destroying my Nikki because she'll realize that I've kept the facts to myself once my printed words are shared with the public. She'll cry because she'll learn that what I've been carrying on my own is much more burdensome than she ever knew. She'll break at just the idea of what I've battled with internally. She'll hurt as my dearest friend. She'll feel for me like anyone would feel for someone they've bonded with and deeply cared about for so long.

Nikki's voicemail begins to play, and a strange and unexpected feeling comes over me, a slight calm, something that I never feel when I can't reach her. I don't know what I had in mind to say to her when my fingers rushed to dial her, but I'm much more at ease knowing that I'll be leaving something for her to return to, something that'll hopefully bring a smile to her face at some point.

I wipe my face though she won't be able to see it. I clear my throat, make sure my words will be heard. Just my words and not my hurt. I massage my throat until I hear the beep. After I do, I open my mouth and prepare to speak. In an instant, the pain returns to my throat. I pull the phone from my ear, rub my neck roughly, take a full breath in, and release it. I feel some comfort, enough to speak, enough to get out all I need to say to Nikki. I bring the phone back to my ear, breathe in and exhale again. "It's me," I say. "I just wanted to tell you that I love you. I love you more than I've ever loved anyone." I remove the phone from my ear, prepare to press end, then remember to thank her, to thank her for something I didn't expect at all today. With the phone pressed against my ear again, I say, "Thank you, Nikki. Thank you for giving me my last laugh."

I end the call, let my phone drop to the floor, and my head fall back against the bed. The sharp pain returns, and without trying to massage it away, without trying to get rid of what won't stay away, I endure it. I experience just another form of what I live through daily. Suffering.

My body shifts violently. My teeth begin to chatter. Just like before, I get smacked with an unexpected case of the chills.

I push myself up to my feet. Haunting memories filled with disturbing images have turned my mind into the most horrifying place. A place I can't simply lock and stay out of, but instead am trapped inside. My anxieties and post-traumatic symptoms have transformed my body into an out of my control frame that I exist within, and like my mind, can't escape. Without warning, without the ability to stop what's happening, I can go from shaking to blacking out, from feeling like a furnace to feeling like a freezer. I can't control my mental or physical state. While an outsider may simply suggest a change of scenery, a change of habit, or something to that effect, I'm expected to be in court tomorrow morning, where my life and tragedy will be the entire focus. Not only can I not bear to sit and listen to the opinions and false conclusions of strangers, but I don't want the guilty or the accused to be convicted.

Shivering, the ache in my throat still there, I grab the dictionary, the thesaurus, a phone book that my aunt has had for over a decade and carry them with trembling hands into the closet. I stack them on top of the quilt and pillows before looking up again, before realizing I need more height.

Boxes filled with old books were stored in this room when I had first moved in to recover. After several long months of looking up at that square, I had finally decided to see what was above me, hidden in the ceiling. Left to myself for hours one Sunday afternoon, while Aunt Linda was praising in church, I moved slowly about the room, repeatedly doing my deep breathing exercises, and preparing myself for some heavy lifting. Unrushed, I was able to push each box, take needed breaks, sip some water, breathe a little more, until I finally felt prepared enough to lift the smaller box filled with thick books and stack it on top of the other. A two-box stack would've been simple for another guy my age to assemble, but the weight and the fear of hurting myself, though I was physically recovering smoothly, drew the process out. It took longer than expected, but I was determined to satisfy my unwavering curiosity.

Two boxes, the one on top not as wide, created something sturdy enough to easily climb, and high enough for me to finally take a peek. I stood atop them with my phone in one hand, and with the other, knocked on the ceiling twice to scare off any four-legged creatures that may have been nesting near the entrance. Then, I pushed the wooden square up and over.

Choking began immediately. The second my head cleared the opening, the overwhelming smell of old, musty dust crashed into my face like an unexpected wave.

Still coughing like an asthmatic, still standing, I used my phone as a flashlight. Countless wooden posts made the small space look like an unfinished structure, impracticable for storing even small things. I had quickly realized why it had been left abandoned, untouched, and unmentioned by Aunt Linda. To her, the space is pointless, an area of her home she can't even reach. For me, it didn't seem so useless. The posts, the location, my life, all combined gave me an idea, an unpleasant thought, but a potential way out. A fast and much-needed escape plan.

With my mind made up, I dropped my phone, hopped down from the boxes, and stepped into Aunt Linda's room. Like my mother, and every other woman in this town, my aunt had and still has countless pairs of pantyhose and tights stored in her top drawer. While I'm sure millennials are unfamiliar with them, the ladies in this town wouldn't dare enter a church without them. They're an essential component of any polished woman's outfit, so over time, their collections grow.

Before digging through her drawer, I had checked her wastebasket, hoping to find a pair or two she'd discarded. Unsurprisingly, there weren't any. In this house, everything is reusable. I didn't see the point in looking around for them. She had likely cut them up and found various uses for pairs she could no longer wear due to runs or holes. Uses like moth ball holders or dusters. So instead of searching for cut up hosiery being multipurposed around the house, I opened her drawer, and selected three of her thickest pairs of tights, as her sheer pantyhose wouldn't do much good.

I stepped back across the hall, fisting the three pairs I was prepared to find another use for that very afternoon. But my phone rang, blaring out a ringtone that's always been assigned to one specific caller. I stepped back into the closet, found it right beside the stacked boxes, and answered Nikki. She had lied about feeling ill to get out of church service early because she wanted to spend the afternoon with me. Her call called off my plan.

I couldn't let Nikki find me that way, couldn't allow her to think she had made it just a minute too late, so while waiting for her to arrive, I climbed back up the stack, tossed the tights into the dark space in the ceiling, and sat patiently.

I didn't move the boxes. I'd felt too overwhelmed with emotion after her call to move too much more. I remember feeling touched that she had lied to be with me that afternoon, but I also felt disappointed because I knew I'd have to face the evening without her when she'd have to leave. I felt terrified of the thoughts that'd be waiting to cycle through my mind once she could no longer distract me. I remember feeling frustrated that my perfect opportunity had been interrupted, but I was still heartened by the fact that it was Nikki who had killed my plan.

Once she arrived, she decided to take a look in the ceiling, even considered climbing in to see if anything was hidden up there before sitting to chat with me, but she never climbed in. She took a quick look that lasted just a few seconds, as she found the smell too much to handle, stated surely that it was mold as opposed to dust, and hurried to move the wooden square back into place.

Once Nikki hopped down, she declined my assistance and struggled to push the boxes back out of the closet on her own, while scolding me for moving them in the first place. I promised never to touch them again, and I never got the chance to. I'll be able to keep that promise even tonight because they're no longer in the room. Tonight, I'll have to make something else work.

I step back out the closet, my mind back on this night, my hands still quivering, body still begging for heat, pain still trapped in my throat. I look around for what could take the place of the boxes that allowed me to reach the ceiling before. Though their presence never bothered me and didn't make me feel like I was forced to live in a storage space, my Aunt and Nikki struggled to push them out of the room to create more space and make where I slept appear more welcoming.

Boxes gone. No convenient ladder. Not enough books to get me up there. I turn, rub my neck, look around for what I could potentially make use of. The small dresser grabs my eye. Like most of the other furniture in this house, it's been here for years. I question what it can hold as far as weight, knock on it twice, feel discouraged by the sound of hollowness, but begin to push it toward the closet anyway. My weight may prove too much for the old piece of bedroom furniture, but I don't need it to hold me for long.

The sound of pushing the wood dresser across her wood floors makes me pause. Old, they may be, but this is Aunt Linda's home, and these are her floors. Already, she'll be tasked with something no one should be tasked with come morning. She'll have to discover me, walk in on a scene that she'll be incapable of erasing from her mind. *Ever*. She'll be the one who has to call in what she finds. She'll have to tell my parents, start the spreading of the news. That's more than enough, and I feel awful that I'm placing all of that in her lap to deal with. The least I can do is spare her floors, stop pushing before deep scratches appear. It's not much of a gift in comparison to what she'll have to face tomorrow morning, but in time, my absence will make life easier for her, too. I'm related to her, tied to her, and like my parents, my sexuality has created difficulty in her life as well. Having a gay nephew in a town this small, this traditional, this close-minded, earns her as much judgment as it does prayer. They don't believe one can be born gay, so the only people left to blame are me, *the disappointing homosexual,* and my relatives as they must've done something wrong. While it's not something our neighbors come right out and say because of my father's position in the church, it's something my parents and aunt feel, something they can't escape because I'm still here.

I pull the top drawer out slightly. Before attempting to grip the piece of furniture, I open and close my fists twice. There are only a few garments inside, so I know it won't be dreadfully heavy, but I don't want to lose my hold. I've been feeling unstable all day. My body has been fighting through emotional and physical strife from the moment I woke up this morning. I may only have to move this dresser a few short feet, but dropping it is going to create too loud of a bang for my aunt and parents to ignore.

It does pain my heart that I haven't been peeked in on, especially because I know Aunt Linda would've at least asked if I'm okay by now if my parents weren't out front with her. It does burn to be reminded so frequently that I'm at the bottom of everyone's list, if I have a place on the list at all. It's a reality that covers me in a feeling I wouldn't wish on anyone, not even those who've made me feel this way. To feel meaningless, like utter garbage, and nothing more than a viral story for the rest of the world to follow and judge is something I can't wait to end. This pain in my throat is something I can't wait to be relieved of. The swirling horror show in my mind is something I can't wait to cut off. My life, that of a homosexual teen residing in a tiny, southern, small-minded community is something I'm ready to end. I've gone from consciousness to blacking out, from hot to cold, from calm to frantic, from relief to excruciating pain, from certainty to reaching out to Nikki.

No more doubt. No more suffering. No interruptions allowed. No time to waste. This is it. This is the night before the trial. My love is with Nikki. A constant reminder is in her voicemail to replay as occasional or as often as she needs to hear it. My truth is printed. I can only pray it frees Bruce and keeps my father out of prison and with my mother who needs him more than she does me.

Being removed by the authorities in the morning will give Aunt Linda her home and life back. I hate knowing the sight of me will be traumatic, but I believe she'll heal and will feel so much lighter no longer being tasked with cooking for me every day, getting me to my appointments, fulfilling roles that my mother decided not to, and sharing her table with someone who had sex with a man.

Me, well, I don't know what's waiting for me on the other side. My decision is far from a holy one, but it feels like the only one. I just know I can't survive another hour feeling like this, let alone make it through the entire trial, day in and day out being in the spotlight, and having so much of my life and character turned upside down and any other way to prove a case relying on so few facts. I just can't. Continuing on, seeing where things end, waiting to see where I go from here is a scarier thought than the images my mind won't free me of. I always come back to this very idea, the fantasy of being removed from all of this, of being erased from this entire mess known as my life. That's because it's the only thing that'll truly free me and those who are in this web with me.

I grip the dresser, lift it, grunt as I move it the short distance to the closet. I set it down, hurriedly move the books, quilt, and pillows from where they're sitting, directly beneath the square. I inch the dresser over in their place, push the top drawer in, and place the dictionary, the thesaurus, and the phone book on top. The added height won't only prove helpful and make setting up easier for me, but it'll give me something to kick over.

The pain in my throat becomes a knot, one that requires a hard, emotional cry to ease. I feel what my body is begging for me to do, but I don't stop to break. I'm tired of breaking down, tired of crying, tired of pain altogether. I'm not putting this off for even a few extra minutes. I'm not going to give my body the chance to fall weak again and render me incapable of finishing this. I'm so close. For the first time in so very long, I can say with certainty that what I'm feeling won't last much longer.

I step out of the closet, back into the room, and grab my phone, what'll work as my flashlight again. Without pausing, I move back into the closet, step on the pillows and quilt, push up onto the dresser, don't let the sound of creaking wood make me pause for even a moment, step on top of the three books, and push the square up and over. I grab a pair of tights from the small pile of three bunched together. I sit my phone face up next to the pile, giving the dark, unfinished space a glow.

I stretch out the pair before pushing up on my tiptoes to reach the closest wooden post, about a foot and a half away from the opening. I wrap the hosiery around the post multiple times before knotting it securely three times.

I don't believe suicide should be a part of anyone's prayer, so I make silent wishes instead for the tights to hold strong, to not fail me as they don't need to hold me for long. According to my research, I'll lose consciousness in seconds, and brain death will occur only minutes later.

I touch my phone screen, make sure the light doesn't dim, and then create a loose knot in the middle of the leg and another knot closer to the end, near the feet of the pair.

I tap my phone screen again, keep my light on, ensure I don't lose visibility as I grab another pair. With the second pair of tights in hand, I stand atop the books, no longer raised on my toes, and stretch the nylon out.

With the top of the pair in hand, I push up on my tiptoes again, and force it through the loose knot I formed in the middle of the first pair. I give the first pair that's tied to the post a strong tug, tightening up the knot to make for certain it holds on to the second pair securely. I release the first pair, tie and pull the top of the second pair several times, forming a thick, hard knot beside the one I made in the first pair.

The space goes dark. I release the second pair, come down off my toes, and take a deep breath. It's not a cleansing one, not a calming one, not one that proves even slightly helpful in easing the sharpness stabbing me in the throat from the inside. Just a breath my body forced me to take without bringing about any benefits.

I begin to shake, begin to feel a heatwave coming over me again, a flash fire of so many emotions, burning my skin, stifling me.

No time. No time to let it get the best of me, the last of me. There'll be no strength left in me to finish this if I allow another surge of unbeatable emotions to run through me, and ultimately, run over me.

On my tiptoes one final time, I bring light back to the space. I repeat the same process I did before, but this time with the second loose knot I made in the first pair. With what's left of the second pair, I tie a small makeshift noose. Repeatedly, I knot it, until my sweaty, jittery hands can't work anymore. I've done something so many times in the last few minutes that I never had the pleasure of doing even once in my life. I tied knot after knot to seal my fate, but never got to, and never will have the pleasure of tying the knot with a man I love. Something I once believed I'd do with Bruce.

I grab my phone, light no longer needed, and toss it down onto the quilt and pillows below. Shaking all over, I force the tightly knotted noose over my head. I can feel the hold, but standing on my toes, still supported by the books, it can't do what I created it to do.

With my right foot, I nudge the books so they fall upon the softness of the bedding below.

Nothing to stand on. No turning back. *I'm sorry, Aunt Linda. God, please forgive me.*

It takes seconds for me to lose all feeling in my body, to be rid of all physical pain. Hopefully, it'll only take a few seconds more to get me out of my head. The sound of my pounding heartbeat floods me with guilt for what I've decided to do. The only way to free myself is one of the greatest ways to go against my religion.

Light begins to fade, not because of a sudden loss of power, not because the space suddenly went pitch black, but because my consciousness is going, because my life is leaving my body, because I'm asphyxiating.

My phone begins to ring. The sound is so distant, almost a whisper. My vision is gone, my hearing nearly lost too, as in only seconds I'm almost completely unconscious. Still, the faint tune can be made out. It's a ringtone that belongs to only one person, that's assigned to only one caller, that always lets me know who's calling without me having to look at the screen. It's the last sound I'll ever hear. The caller is the one and only person who has consistently shown me the meaning of true love, right up until the end. *My Nikki*

Acknowledgements

There are so many people who played a role in helping me publish this novella. Each of you mean so much to me.

As always, first and foremost, I must thank God for all the blessings He has bestowed upon me. I am still struggling with my anxiety, but I've never felt abandoned. I give full thanks to my Heavenly Father for helping me to go on, to keep fighting, to keep writing, and most of all, to keep smiling.

Kayla and Kaden, you mean everything to mommy. I look at your faces and I feel a fire that motivates me to work a little harder, to be a little braver, to take on another challenge. I want to make you both so proud. I want you both to see me achieve my goals, knowing that you can do the same, no matter what obstacles stand in your way. I could never fully explain just how privileged and blessed I feel to be your mother. I love you more than these words, more than anything, more than anyone else on this planet ever could.

Thierry "T" Arnoux. I owe you fifty thank

yous. I can't count how many passages I read to you, how many times I asked what you thought of a certain character, a certain line, etc. Never did you try to shut me up. Never did you lie. You encouraged me to keep writing and really applauded me for being brave enough to create something so dark. I appreciate that, and I appreciate you for never allowing me to doubt myself. I also appreciate you holding my hand so tightly during one of the scariest times of my life. Thank you for everything.

Kahina "Bubbles/ Bubbs" Haynes, there's no way I couldn't thank you for listening to me go on and on about this project. Though I was purposely vague, your excitement about what I was comfortable sharing made me feel so much more confident about it. Thank you for always being there, and for calling me "Lady Gaga".

Stephane "Oh yeah" Arnoux, I owe you a huge thank you, too. Sitting in your kitchen and going on about this project, with you listening and even offering to come to any of my events, meant everything for me. So, I couldn't write this and not thank you for your love and support. It means more than I could say.

Holly, it was such a pleasure to work with you again. Your detailed critique really helped me to improve upon this story. You're an amazing beta-reader, and I fully appreciate the detail you continue to give to my work. I look forward to working with you again.

Dominique, I knew we'd work together again, and I'm so glad we got to for this project. I truly appreciate your eye for detail. You caught errors I missed after several readthroughs. I am so grateful for you and I know we'll work together again on future projects. You're incredible at what you do. Thank you for everything!

Harley Lyn, I am so glad I found you. You were amazing to work with. Not only did you catch the errors I'd never want my readers to stumble over, but you also proofread this piece in record time. I am so happy we got to work together, and I hope we get to again. You're a Rockstar! Thank you for everything.

Erin Dunagan, I am so happy I decided to hire you. My gut never lies, and it told me that there were a few errors that slipped past all of us. I was right, and thankfully, your skilled eye caught them. I really appreciate your hard work and your unbelievably fast turnaround time. Thank you so much. It was an absolute pleasure working with you. You're fantastic!

The Book Khaleesi, I can't thank you enough. From cover design to formatting, you've got me covered. I have worked with you on every one of my projects, and I've never been disappointed, not even slightly. Your timeliness, kindness, professionalism, and knowledge always make me return to you confidently. I feel so blessed to have found you years ago, and no doubt, I'll be back. Eeva, you're just amazing!

Last, but certainly not least, I have to thank all of my family and friends. I love and appreciate you all. Just asking about my writing touches my heart. Thank you so much for the love and support.

Thank you all for helping me make my dream come true!